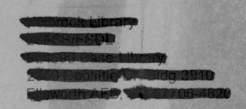

WILLIAM
SHATNER

Tek
Kill

AN ACE • PUTNAM BOOK

PUBLISHED BY G. P. PUTNAM'S SONS
NEW YORK

An Ace/Putnam Book

Published by G. P. Putnam's Sons

Publishers Since 1838

200 Madison Avenue

New York, NY 10016

Library of Congress Cataloging-in-Publication Data

Shatner, William.

Tek kill / by William Shatner.

p.   cm.

ISBN 0-399-14202-9 (alk. paper)

1. Cardigan, Jake (Fictitious character)—Fiction.

2. Private investigators—Fiction.   I. Title.

PS3569.H347T413   1996   96-19992 CIP

813'.54—dc20

Printed in the United States of America

1   3   5   7   9   10   8   6   4   2

This book is printed on acid-free paper. ∞

Book design by Julie Duquet

I would like to acknowledge

CARMEN LaVIA
SUSAN ALLISON
IVY FISCHER STONE

I'd like to dedicate this book to Ron Goulart. Mining the words out of a rich vein of plot— a miner, but no minor, his face blackened with printer's ink, his fingers blue with bruises from the keyboard—he toils in unrecognized effort. Hail to you, Ronald, a writer of minor physique but of major talent.

1 • LAT_E

on the night of February 3, 2122, she saw them murder her brother.

Saw it clearly inside her head while she huddled, hugging herself with her thin arms, in the deep armchair in the big domed redwood-and-plastiglass bedroom where she spent most of her time now. All the long days and nights.

When the vision, sudden and unbidden, hazy at first, started, Susan Grossman jerked upright. Pressing her right hand hard to her left breast, she inhaled sharply. As her slim body began shaking, the dark-haired young woman could hear her heart thumping in her ears.

Susan had been hoping she wouldn't have any more of these seizures or whatever they were.

"Not another one," she murmured in a low, sad voice. "Please, no more."

She shut her eyes, even though she knew that wouldn't help. She'd have to suffer through the painful, unwanted vision anyway. That was always the way it was.

What she saw now, quite clearly, was her brother Dwight outside in the large holographic garden at the back of his half-acre estate over in the Woodland Hills Sector of Greater Los Angeles. A lean, dark man of thirty-seven, nearly seventeen years older than his sister, he was standing in the slightly hunched way of his. He faced a heavyset man who had absolutely no hair on his head or face. Not even eyebrows.

The hairless man was arguing with her brother, his skin glowing deathly white in the light from the globes floating over the night garden.

She heard Dwight tell him, "You really don't think that's going to work, do you?"

"It's a very reasonable offer, sir." The man's voice was high-pitched, piping.

"Just leave now," ordered Dwight Grossman. "Get the hell away from here."

"I'm really terribly sorry this turned out this way, sir."

A second man, unseen by her brother, appeared behind him. In his knobby left hand he held a snub-nosed lazgun.

"Dwight, look out!" she cried, rising up from her chair.

Her head was throbbing, pain zigzagged through her lean body. This was worse than any Tek spasm she'd ever experienced.

The second man—small, frail, and red-haired—fired the gun. The beam went digging into her brother's back, slashing through cloth and then flesh.

Dirty gray smoke came spurting up as Dwight screamed, doubling, and toppled forward.

Susan could smell the deep, black wound.

The hairless man moved aside as Dwight, a large bloody rut smoking across his back, fell down into a projected rosebush. The image of red blossoms closed in around his sprawled body.

The hairless man smiled, nodding satisfaction. "That was nicely done," he told the little redheaded man.

SOMETIME AFTER MIDNIGHT Susan finally forced herself to leave her room. She had no phone of her own. Her father felt she wasn't ready for one again just yet.

Moving slowly and quietly along the dimlit upper hallway, the thin young woman headed for the stair ramp leading down to the lower level of the Bel Air Sector mansion. All you could hear in the night house was the hum of the various mechanisms that ran the place and the chill wind that was blowing down across the hills outside.

Susan was fairly certain her father had turned in earlier. She didn't want to encounter him. He wouldn't understand what she'd experienced tonight.

"Say I had a relapse," she murmured. "Tell me I had to go away again."

She made her way, cautiously, down the curving ramp.

Susan didn't want to run into the woman her father was currently living with, either.

"She thinks I'm nothing but a crazy Tekhead. She'd call Dr. Stolzer for sure."

Dr. Stolzer would mean going back to that grim, dead-white rehab facility out in the Palm Springs Sector. Being hooked up to all those awful gadgets and having those damned medbots always hovering around and talking to you in their tinny patronizing voices.

Sometimes, most times, it was really damn hard not to ease back into the old ways. Hook up to a Brainbox, drop a Tek chip, and get clean away from all this shit.

Shaking her head, Susan pushed open the door of the library.

"Low light," she whispered.

The room obliged and became faintly illuminated.

For some reason she was having trouble breathing now. She couldn't seem to take a deep breath and her ribs were hurting.

Hurrying to the vidphone table, Susan seated herself. Carefully she punched out her brother's number.

There was no guarantee that the latest vision was true. All the others had proven to be accurate. But maybe this one wasn't.

The phonescreen remained black.

"Let him be alive," she said softly as she tried the number once again.

Nothing happened. She didn't get her brother's recorded answering image, nor did any of his bot servants show up on the phonescreen.

She sat back in the chair, the breath wheezing in her chest.

Then, making up her mind, she leaned forward to call some-one else.

2

AT five-thirty that morning, Walt Bascom was arrested for the murder of Dwight Grossman.

The chief of the Cosmos Detective Agency had been asleep, alone, in the oval master bedroom of his seaside home in the Santa Monica Sector of Greater LA.

Bright yellow light suddenly blossomed all around him.

Wide awake, the wiry Bascom sat up and reached for his bedside lazgun.

"Don't," someone suggested, clutching his wrist in a rough grip.

He found himself surrounded by five SoCal Police officers. All of them in uniform except Detective Lieutenant Len Drexler, who had hold of him.

Some of the room's windows had been opened, and swirling streamers of white dawn mist were drifting in.

A lean black man, Drexler was wearing a gray suit and holding a lazgun aimed at him. "Morning, Walt," he said, letting go and inching back. "We've dropped over to arrest you."

"For what, Drexler?" He swung his legs out of the bed and sat on its edge. "Must be serious if it requires five goons."

One of the uniformed cops gave an annoyed grunt and scooped Bascom's silvery lazgun off the night table.

"Eleven goons actually," corrected the police detective. "The rest of them are searching the place. One of them is confiscating your secsystem vidtapes."

"You've got all the necessary warrants?"

Perching on the foot of the wide bed, Wexler grinned and patted a jacket pocket. "I can show them to you, Walt," he offered.

"Never mind," said Bascom, wiggling his toes a couple of times. "But you might tell me what you're arresting me for."

"Dwight Grossman was killed around about midnight."

"No great loss. And?"

"We have reason to believe you committed the murder."

"Bullshit," suggested the agency chief, standing up. He was wearing the top half of a candy-striped pair of pajamas. "I've been here since a little after eleven-thirty. Hell, the tapes your boy is grabbing will establish that."

"And where do you claim you were earlier tonight?" asked the policeman, getting up from the rumpled bed and keeping his weapon trained on the detective agency chief.

"I claim I was exactly where I really was." Bascom was frowning at the black detective. "I had a date with Kay Norwood. We——"

"A very respectable attorney," observed Drexler.

"Too respectable for me, huh?" Bascom gave a small impatient sigh. "Anyway, Lieutenant, Kay and I went to dinner in the Studio City Sector," he continued. "She's preparing a case, wanted to get home fairly early. I left her at her place around eleven and came back here."

"Witnesses?" inquired Drexler.

"I live alone, except for Ambrose, my android valet and handyman. But he can tell you what time I got here."

The lieutenant shook his head and attempted to look sad. "Is Ambrose that chrome-plated andy in the white suit?"

"Yeah. What did—"

"Poor guy seems to have had some kind of accident," explained Drexler. "He's spread-eagled flat on his ass in your pantry, Walt."

One of the cops chuckled.

"You assholes used a disabler on him," accused Bascom, angry, jabbing a finger in the lieutenant's direction.

"You know that would be illegal." He shrugged and another of his men laughed. "What I'm trying to convey, Walt, is that this andy—Ambrose, is it?—poor old Ambrose is out of commission and isn't going to be able to back up any of your statements. Damn shame."

"The SoCal cops are going to get the repair bill."

"Seems to me you've got much more important matters to worry about."

Bascom gestured at a dark robe that was hanging over the back of a tin slingchair. "Can I put that on before I freeze my fanny?"

"Sure, but do it slowly and with no funny stuff."

One of the cops took a step back and swung his lazgun to aim it directly at him as the agency chief bent to grab up the robe.

"I'm a crack shot, but I don't think I'm up to shooting it out with five of you lads," Bascom said. "Besides, I don't keep a gun hidden in this."

Drexler said, "Oh, speaking of security tapes, as we were a while ago, Walt. The ones at Grossman's show *you* shooting the poor bastard smack in the back at exactly 11:53."

"That's goddamn impossible." He hit his palm with his fist.

The cop shrugged. "It is also pretty near impossible to fake a tape like that," he said. "We're going to have to arrest you, Walt."

"What, just out of curiosity, would my motive be?"

"Well, Dwight Grossman used to date your friend Kay Norwood before you cut him out," answered Lieutenant Drexler. "Past few weeks he's apparently been calling her, making threats, generally harassing her. Dumb way to try to get her back, but guys do things like that."

"So?"

"So last week at a popular Hollywood Sector bistro you threat-ened to kill the guy if he didn't leave her alone. You put on that little show in front of quite a few attentive bystanders, Walt."

"C'mon. I threatened to poke him in the snoot, not knock him off."

"Not according to what we've heard."

"Does this sound like the kind of slipshod obvious crime I'd commit, Drexler? Give me credit for—"

"You've been pulling all sorts of shady stuff in Greater LA for years, Walt. I think you reached the point long ago where you decided you could get away with just about anything." Nodding at Bascom, Drexler added, "If you don't want to go downtown in your robe, Walt, this would be a damn good time to get some clothes on."

.   .   .

ALTHOUGH HE NEARLY got into a fight a little over an hour
later, Jake Cardigan woke up a few minutes beyond seven A.M.
feeling neither angry nor apprehensive. When he stepped out
onto the moderately foggy deck of the Malibu Sector condo he
shared with his son, he found Dan already sitting at the breakfast
table finishing up a plazcup of orangesub.

Dan, a lanky young man of sixteen, was already dressed in his
SoCal Police Academy uniform. "Morning," he said, smiling.

"Is that a smirk?" Jake sat opposite and glanced out across the
yellow sand at the pale, blurred Pacific.

"Nope, just a simple filial grin," Dan assured him. "It probably
has nothing to do with the fact that you didn't return from your
date with Bev Kendricks until nearly two A.M."

"Wasn't exactly a date." Jake poured himself a cup of nearcaf.
"Bev and I attended a symposium on the latest developments in
forensic robots and—"

"That's some symposium that lasted until the wee hours."

"There were a lot of audience questions afterward."

"Well, if you're not seriously romancing Bev by this time, Dad,
you ought to be."

"Bev's a private investigator and I'm a private investigator, and
that gives us a basis for a friendship." He shook his head. "This
isn't exactly a romance yet."

"You've been using that 'we're just colleagues' dodge for
months."

Jake sipped his nearcaf. "What about you and Molly Fine? Is
that still a romance?"

Smiling, Dan answered, "It sure is. We're colleagues, too—
both police acad cadets—but I don't hide behind that."

"Proving that youth is not as complicated as age."

"We're more honest and open, sure."

Jake rested an elbow on the table. "I really am making an effort to get socially involved with people," he quietly told his son. "To you it probably seems that Beth Kittredge has been dead for a hell of a long time. To me, though . . . I still sometimes have the feeling she was killed only a few days ago."

Dan nodded, saying, "I know, Dad. And I'm not trying to interfere in your life. It's only that—"

"I'm still moping and brooding too much."

"Somewhat," agreed his son.

"I really am working at it." Jake leaned back in his chair, looked up into the hazy morning, and then grinned. "It appears Gomez is descending on us."

His partner's familiar skycar was dropping down toward the landing area beside the condo building.

"Good," said Dan. "He'll cheer you up."

But that didn't turn out to be so.

3 ● BASCOM

wouldn't murder anybody," observed Jake as the skycar climbed up through the hazy morning. "No, let's amend that. He wouldn't murder anybody in such a clumsy, unsubtle way. Hell, there wouldn't be clues, wouldn't be sectapes of his doing the deed."

"*Sí,* exactly," agreed Sid Gomez, who was in the pilot seat. "However, your old *compañero* Lieutenant Drexler believes otherwise. Which is why our esteemed *jefe* is residing in the hoosegow at the moment."

"It's got to be a frame-up."

Gomez, who was roughly ten years younger than his partner, nodded. "A very thorough one, though," he pointed out. "From what I've been able to glean, the security camera stuff looks *and* tests absolutely authentic. Far as the minions of the law can tell, anyway."

"But that security footage can't be legit." Slouching in his seat, Jake absently massaged the knuckles of his left hand.

"Proving that is only one of several jobs facing the Cosmos Detective Agency."

"Now, about some more background on this emergency meeting you're dragging me to?"

"A strategy session, *amigo.* We have to start working on this whole mess even while Bascom is still in the clink."

"You haven't mentioned," said Jake, "who's running the agency while Bascom's away."

Stroking his bushy mustache, Gomez squinted out at the brightening morning. "I was hoping I could get you safely delivered to work without that particular name crossing my rose-petal lips."

Jake sat up. "Bascom put Roy Anselmo in as acting chief, huh?"

"Well, *sí.* I know you think Roy is a pompous, egotistic putz, yet he—"

"You," reminded Jake, "share my opinion of the guy, Sidney."

"Okay, we're unanimous as to his being a pompous putz. But the *hombré,* even you must admit, is an efficient operative and a damn good administrator."

"Maybe."

"You weren't expecting the *jefe* to put you in charge, were you?"

"Jesus, no." Jake stiffened further, shaking his head and frowning. "But I can sure as hell think of a lot of people at the Cosmos Agency I'd rather have bossing me. I can even draw up a list of lesser assholes I'd prefer."

"Well, *amigo*, we must repress our true feelings and concentrate on saving Bascom's ass," urged his partner. "So, *por
favor*, control your dislike for Roy when we arrive at this
get-together."

"I'll behave," promised Jake with minimal conviction.

4 • D

An narrowed his left eye and studied the slim, dark-haired young woman who stood beside the skycar. "You don't believe any of that, do you, Molly?"

"I sort of think I do. Especially after last night." Molly Fine made an impatient gesture that urged him to climb aboard. "Get in or we'll be late."

Dan circled the vehicle and climbed into the passenger seat. "This Susan Grossman is a recovering Tek addict, isn't she?"

"She is, yes," admitted Molly as she took the controls of the skycar. "But she's off Tek now and what she—"

"Go back, slowly," requested Dan, "and explain just what went on last night."

The car quietly rose up off the morning beach.

Molly said, "Just shy of midnight Sue saw this image. Well, it was some kind of telepathic vision, sort of."

"Okay, let's pause for comments from the audience," Dan cut in. "I don't believe there's any such thing as a telepathic vision."

"Sure, there is. Matter of fact, Sue's experienced several over the past few weeks. Just about all of them, from what I've been able to determine, turned out to be accurate."

"You never mentioned any of this to me, Molly."

"Well, that's mostly because I anticipated your skeptical reaction."

"And this vision she claims to have had last night isn't the only one, then?"

"Susan seems to have developed an ability a few weeks ago. She confided in me about what was happening to her," explained Molly as the skycar climbed to an altitude of 5,000 feet.

"This time she saw her brother being murdered?"

Molly answered, "That's what I've been telling you. Sue still isn't in terrific shape and she's pretty much afraid of her father and the dreadful woman he's got living with him. That's why she waited awhile before getting up the nerve to go downstairs to phone her brother and check on—"

"She doesn't have a phone in her room?"

"Her father doesn't think she's ready for one yet."

"How old is she?"

"Around twenty."

"What you're putting your faith in is a full-grown woman who isn't trustworthy enough to be allowed near a vidphone or—"

"You have to know her father to understand the setup. He's extremely protective of her."

Dan said, "Okay, go back to what happened."

"Susan tried to phone her brother's place, twice. But there was no answer, not even from a bot servant."

The car sped on across the morning, aimed for the SoCal Police Academy.

"Did she call the law next?"

"No, she phoned me," replied Molly. "She knew they'd react the way you have. You know, decide this was just a Tekkie having another hallucination."

"Then you sent the police to Dwight Grossman's?"

"Actually, I only asked somebody to check and see if her brother was okay," she said. "They went there and found he'd been killed."

"You know they arrested Walt Bascom, my dad's boss, for the killing, don't you?"

"Yes, but Bascom didn't have a darn thing to do with it," she assured him. "Sue saw the killers."

"In this mystical vision, huh?"

"She clearly saw two men, neither one of them Bascom, do away with Dwight Grossman."

"Somebody going into a trance," mentioned Dan, "and having hallucinations doesn't make for the sort of evidence that stands up in court, Molly."

Molly gave him a corrective jab in the ribs with her right fist. "Don't be so darned narrow-minded, Daniel dear," she advised. "The point to grasp with your peanut brain is that Susan *saw* these guys. We'll be able to provide your father with identifications and holographic mug shots."

"Oh, so? How do we do that? More hoodoo?"

Molly made an impatient noise. "I love you, but sometimes I really wonder about your reasoning abilities," she admitted. "As soon as we arrive at the police academy, we'll drop in at the Background & ID room and consult with our robot buddy, Rex/GK-30.

Working with the detailed descriptions I got out of Sue, Rex'll be able to tap police files and—"

"We're not supposed to use Rex that way anymore. Remember what—"

"Hooey," observed Molly. "If we're going to help get Bascom out of the jug, we'll have to take a few small risks."

"Getting expelled isn't exactly a small risk," he told her. "Besides, we have classes all—"

"We can miss Lieutenant Cutler's Electronic Forensics 22B lecture today," Molly said confidently.

"I suppose," said Dan, slumping in his seat.

The skycar flew on toward the Santa Monica Sector.

5 • THE

top of Bascom's desk looked much neater than usual and all the windows of his large tower office had been unblanked, affording an unobstructed view of the metal-and-plastiglass buildings rising up all around out in the early-morning haze. Seated at the desk of the absent chief of the Cosmos Detective Agency was a husky man with feathery blond hair. He held his voxwatch to his ear as Gomez and Jake made their way up to take seats facing the desk. "This emergency meeting was scheduled for 8:15 on the nose, fellas," he mentioned.

"*¡Caramba!* And here we come dragging in at the ungodly hour of 8:22." Gomez slumped into a tin slingchair.

"In point of fact, it's almost 8:30, but we'll let that pass."

Anselmo smiled a forgiving smile. "We have considerable ground to cover, so let's not waste any more time getting under way."

"In point of fact," offered Jake from the plastiglass chair he'd settled into, "it's my fault we're so late, Roy. I was the one who insisted we get into a drag race with a skyvan that was done up to resemble a tofu burger and—"

"Your flippant attitude is really out of place at a serious meeting like this, Jake," Anselmo told him.

Gomez leaned back and rested a booted foot on the edge of the hologram projection stage. "Get on with your sermon, *por favor.*"

A slim Japanese woman sitting immediately to the rear of Gomez made an annoyed clucking sound. "Get your feet off the equipment."

"You need a lube job, Karin," he said, not bothering to look over his shoulder at her. "That's what's causing that rusty noise you're continually—Ah, I forgot. You're not really a robot or an andy, you merely behave like one."

"Sid," said Anselmo from behind his boss's desk, "we're all here this morning to help Walt Bascom out of this little jam he's—"

"Getting tossed in the *calabozo* and charged with murder ranks a shade higher than a little jam."

Karin Tanoshi made her noise again. "I was against Cardigan and Gomez being invited," she said, anger in her thin voice. "They're both behaving like—"

"Please, Karin," Anselmo came in. "Keep in mind, dear, that I'm following Walt Bascom's wishes in all this."

There were three other Cosmos operatives at the meeting, two men and a woman. The larger of the men said now, "Why don't you quit the bickering, Roy, and get on with it?"

"A good suggestion, Anson." The thickset blond detective rose to his feet, rested his palms atop the freshly polished desk. "Let me reiterate the fact that this is an extremely serious situation we find ourselves in. The seven of us will comprise the core team that will investigate the Dwight Grossman killing." He paused to cough into his fist. "I'll remind you, so as to make my own position crystal clear, that you were, each one of you, personally selected by Walt. Your names were given to me during the brief vidphone conversation I was allowed to have with the chief earlier this morning."

"He's obviously not thinking clearly." Karin was sitting uneasily on the edge of her chair, fingers twisting around each other.

"Don't fret, *chiquita*," said Gomez. "My name always makes it onto any list of crackerjack private ops."

Anselmo continued, "I also want to assure you folks that I, as I'm completely certain you do, believe completely and totally in Walt Bascom's innocence. We're going to have ourselves, however, one hell of a time proving he didn't commit this brutal murder."

"The SoCal Police already have considerable damning evidence against Mr. Bascom." Karin made her way over to one of the large wall viewscreens.

Anselmo told them, "We've been able to get hold of copies of all the security camera tapes that the police have acquired. Karin, hon, let's see the stuff from the murdered man's home first off."

Karin bent to touch a control panel.

And there was Bascom on the wall, nearly life size. Hair rumpled, suit wrinkled and baggy, he was standing in the middle of a black-and-silver living room. His fists were clenched and Bascom was yelling at the lean, dark younger man facing him a few yards away.

"That's Grossman," said Anselmo.

"I deduced that," said Gomez.

"Pay attention, you crazy bastard," shouted the angry Bascom. "You're going to leave Kay Norwood totally alone. You understand me, asshole?"

"My relationship with Kay is none of your goddamn business," Grossman told him disdainfully.

Moving closer, shoulders hunched in anger, Bascom said, "It is my business. I don't give a shit whether you love her or hate her. But if you ever call her again or threaten her in any way, I'll fix you so you won't be able to bother anybody. Ever."

Grossman shook his head pityingly. "Why don't you face reality, Bascom," he said quietly. "Everybody knows—and, yes, let me assure you, that includes Kay herself—everybody knows you're too old for her." Turning his back, he went striding for the open doorway leading out to the bright holographic garden outside. "Very much too old."

Bascom tugged an ebony lazgun out of a rumpled pocket of his coat.

He ran after the departing Grossman.

Halting on the threshold, he swung the gun up and fired.

The sizzling beam dug into the younger man's narrow back.

"Terrible," gasped Karin as the picture ended.

"What about that gun?" asked Jake.

"It hasn't," answered Anselmo, "been found."

"Walt," observed Leo Anson, shifting in his chair, "would never shoot anybody in the back."

"This is the pertinent footage from Mr. Bascom's home sectapes." Karin touched the panel again.

"You're looking, if I may say so, sir, a trifle seedy," observed the silver-plated, white-suited android who showed on the wallscreen now.

Bascom, even more disheveled than he had been at Grossman's, was crossing his wide yellow-and-white kitchen. "Must be
because I'm in love, Ambrose," he said, his voice raw and raspy.

"May I fix you a nightcap, sir?"

Bascom glanced toward the wall clock. It showed that the time
was 4:06 A.M. "Too late. I'll just turn in."

"Very good, sir," said the mechanical valet. "I trust you'll feel
a bit more chipper come morning."

"No doubt."

The agency wall went blank.

"That's most of what the tapes show," said Anselmo. "Detective Lieutenant Drexler is convinced the footage wasn't faked or
even tampered with."

"Crap," observed Jake. "If Walt really was going to knock
somebody off, he'd know how to disable a secsystem. And he'd
also make damn certain his own tapes didn't catch him pussy-
footing home at the wrong time."

"Sure, that's the logical conclusion," agreed Anselmo. "The
cops, however, are claiming that Walt was so emotionally distraught that he didn't use any caution. Overcome by rage, he
simply went busting into Grossman's."

"Doesn't matter what Drexler says," put in Gomez, "footage
like that can be faked."

"The prelim police tests show no evidence of electronic tam-
pering," said Anselmo. "Even though Walt denies he was ever at
the guy's house, the police are accepting the footage as real."

"What's our own expert, Doc Olan, say?" asked Jake.

"Dr. Olan was rushed copies of this material," said Karin, returning to her seat. "His initial testing shows nothing suspicious."

Gomez was studying the distant ceiling. "I think I'll talk to
some *hombres* who are also experts at this sort of thing," he said.
"Get me copies, Roy."

"There's no need," said Karin, frowning at him, "for you to be showing potentially damaging material like this to your underworld cronies."

Shrugging, Gomez said, "Never mind. I can acquire them on my own."

Anselmo coughed again. "Jake, Bascom wants you to go talk to him at the jailhouse," he said. "I'm obliged to go along with his wishes, although I personally think relying on an ex-con in a situation like this—"

That was as far as the blond detective got.

Jake had left his chair and grabbed hold of the front of his jacket. Lifting the acting head of the Cosmos Detective Agency clear off the floor, he suggested, "I think we ought to forget our personal differences for the duration of this problem, Roy. You quit calling me an ex-con and I'll refrain from booting your fat ass from here to Tuesday."

"Whoa, *momentito.*" Gomez had lunged and caught the angered Karin before she could use her stungun on his partner.

"Okay, all right," said Anselmo as Jake let go of him. "I was probably out of line, Jake."

"Probably, yeah," agreed Jake, taking a slow, deep breath.

"You're right. Walt Bascom's fate is what's important. We're all part of the handpicked team that's going to save his life."

"Sid and I are a team," corrected Jake. "I'll report to you so long as you're in charge, Roy, but I sure as hell don't consider you a teammate."

6 • THE

silver-and-gray elevator dropped swiftly down and down through the underground levels of the SoCal Central Jail in the LA Sector of Greater Los Angeles.

The chill cage hissed to a stop and an overhead voxbox announced, "This is Level 13."

The door whispered open.

"LEFT TO THE VISITOR SCREENING ROOM. HAVE ALL NECESSARY IDENTIFICATION MATERIAL READY."

Jake left the elevator, obligingly turned left, and started along the long gray corridor.

Every two yards, large litesigns on the gray walls reminded, WE

ARE OBLIGED UNDER SOCAL STATE LAW TO INFORM YOU THAT YOU
ARE UNDER CONSTANT ELECTRONIC SURVEILLANCE.

"Thanks for telling me," muttered Jake as he went striding
along.

Two large gunmetal robots stood at the doorway to the
screening room. The one on the left held out his hand, palm up, as
Jake approached. "ID packet with skycar license foremost and
facedown."

As Jake complied, the other big robot began a thorough
frisking. "Mandatory weapons search."

"Your buddies already did one up on Level 1."

"Part of standard procedures." Satisfied, the bot returned to his
position to the right of the door.

"All IDs in order," announced the other mechanical man. "You
are cleared to continue."

"Proceed to the sign-in desk."

Stowing his ID packet back in his pocket, Jake crossed the
threshold.

A slim blond woman in her late twenties was coming toward the
doorway as he entered the big gray room. She came hurrying
forward, took hold of his arm. "So you're one of the ops who's
working on this, huh? He wouldn't tell me." She looked into his
face, frowning some. "Well, I suppose it could be worse."

"I'm surprised to see you hereabouts, Kacey."

Letting go, Kacey Bascom took a step backward. "Oh, sure,
that's right, isn't it?" she said. "Coldhearted conservatives like
me don't care if their father gets tossed in the pokey."

Jake grinned. "You and your pop have been none too close for
as long as I've known him."

"I happen to feel, Jake, that a daughter has a duty to her father,
no matter how crack-brained his political views happen to be,"

she informed him. "He's in very serious trouble and, considering my background in police work and my—"

"Those goons you work for down in the San Diego Sector aren't my notion of cops, Kacey," he told her. "Just about all the under-cover agents in the Political Surveillance Department of the SD Local Police would have to polish up their behavior before even being considered for jobs in a lynch mob. Their ideas of civil rights are—"

"The crime rate down there, and the rate of antigovern-ment activity, is impressively below that of Greater LA," she pointed out.

"You people give witch-hunting a bad name."

Kacey gave an impatient shake of her head. "The point of all this, Jake, is that I'm well schooled in investigative techniques and—"

"Breaking and entering isn't an accepted police procedure in these parts," he said. "Neither is working some poor protester over with a stungun until—"

"Listen, stop ranting," she put in. "I'm not working in San Diego anymore."

"Oh, so? Did they decide you weren't narrow-minded enough for them?"

"I'm in the communications business now, have been for almost six months."

"Communications? What do you do, scrawl hate messages on the sides of churches and—"

"I'm executive assistant to J. J. Bracken."

Jake laughed. "That's perfect, Kacey," he said. "Bracken's the patron saint of all narrowest right-wingers in GLA, and that vidnet show of his, *Facin' Bracken,* is a fount of enough fuzzy-headed claptrap to—"

"J. J. Bracken is a very intelligent and well-informed man,"

Kacey stated. "If people like you, and my equally stubborn father, would listen to him with even a halfway open mind, you'd—"

"I'm here to talk to your father, not get into a pointless debate."

"What I'm struggling to convey to your impenetrable brain, Jake, is that I'm now serving as an investigative reporter for J. J. Bracken. I have a hell of a lot of experience gathering facts."

"Facts? What would Bracken want facts for?"

Kacey clenched her fists at her sides, remaining silent for several seconds. "My father was framed," she said slowly. "He was obviously set up for this murder."

"We agree on that."

She hesitated, then said, "You're probably one of the Cosmos Agency's best operatives, despite your muddled outlook on life. I just now tried to offer my services to my father directly." She sighed. "I'm a damn good cop myself and I know I can dig out the truth. He turned me down." Her hand touched Jake's sleeve. "But if you let—"

"Wait now, Kacey," he said firmly. "I already have a partner— if that's what you're working up to."

"All I want, Jake, is to be able to check in with you regularly," she said hopefully. "And maybe, you know, I could tag along once in a while on the more routine sort of—"

"We can talk occasionally."

"Well, that's a—"

"At a distance and not all that frequently. I'll accept the fact that you're honestly concerned about your dad, but I can't promise a partnership."

"All right, okay. I'll settle for that," Kacey said. "Although I really could be a great help to him and to—"

"I have to see him." He turned away from her and walked over to the sign-in desk.

"Friends of the prisoner consoling each other, was it?" inquired the copper-plated bot behind the desk.

"You've guessed it," answered Jake.

THE GRAY-WALLED CELL was small and contained two gray chairs and a gray cot.

Bascom, looking almost dapper in an unrumpled tan suit, was slowly pacing the gray floor.

Jake, settled in one of the hard metal chairs, said, "Courting Kay Norwood has had a very positive effect on you, Chief. No more wrinkled—" Standing suddenly up, he snapped his fingers.

"Developing a twitch?" inquired the head of the Cosmos Detective Agency, scanning him.

"It just occurred to me that the Bascom on display in all those sectapes is based on the old you. The wrinkled, sloppy Bascom of bygone—"

"Hey, we already know they're faked," cut in Bascom. "What we have to uncover is who did the dirty work."

"And why," added Jake, sitting again. "Any notions on motives for wanting this Grossman fellow dead?"

"Could be he's an innocent bystander. Killed simply to frame me."

"Naw, that's too roundabout a way of doing things," said Jake, shaking his head. "We can look into that angle, but meantime, what about Grossman as a target?"

Bascom took the other chair. "I don't as yet know all that much about the guy, Jake," he admitted. "He worked for the Thelwell Brokerage Services outfit. According to Kay, Grossman specialized in investigating companies and preparing reports on them for would-be investors."

"What sort of companies?"

"Mostly pharmaceutical businesses. Might be an angle there, though I don't see what the hell it is at this juncture."

"What about his private life?"

"Outside of being an obsessive asshole when it came to trying to get Kay to come back into his life," answered the chief, "the late Dwight Grossman was a relatively normal citizen. When he started making trouble—calling her on the vidphone, dropping in at her office—I had the agency run a preliminary check on him."

"And?"

Bascom shrugged. "Sweetness and light for the most part, Jake," he said. "No criminal record, no outstanding debts. He was married once to a respectable lady who's a graphics supervisor at a reputable GLA advertising agency. Divorced, with no fuss and no scandal, two years ago. Mother's dead, father is very well off, and he has a sister who dropped out of college last year. The kid had some sort of mental problems. Seems to have been a breakdown that was pretty likely triggered by a serious Tek addiction."

"Tek," said Jake quietly. "But Grossman himself has no involvement, no connection with the stuff?"

"None that I could unearth. But, again, it's something to dig into further."

"Did you really threaten him?"

"I threatened to coldcock him if he didn't quit harassing Kay." He held up a fist. "I might well have slugged him. But shooting a guy down with a lazgun—nope."

"And you were nowhere near his place last night?"

"Never been there, Jake," he said.

"The security tapes from your house show you coming home around four in the morning," said Jake. "They were faked, obviously, but when were they substituted for the real ones?"

"I've been thinking about that quite a lot," admitted the agency boss. "I never heard a damn thing and no alarm went off.

Ambrose, my valet, was found sprawled on his backside in the kitchen. Could be Drexler and his crew did that, but maybe it was done earlier by parties unknown."

"Lieutenant Drexler is not an especially lovable guy," said Jake, "but I don't see him being directly involved in a frame."

"I wouldn't think so, either," said Bascom. "But we have to check up on him, too. Cops, as shocking as it may seem to a sensitive lad such as you, have been known to sell out for sufficient kale."

"When are you expecting to get out of here?"

"Kay's working on it. Hopefully before sundown."

"Meantime, Sid and I will get going."

Bascom held up his hand. "Couple of more things, Jake," he said. "Firstly, until I'm sprung, please, try to get along with Roy Anselmo."

"We're as friendly as can be, Chief."

"I'm sure, yeah," said Bascom. "And then—well, Kacey dropped in on me right before you called."

"I know, I collided with her outside." He pointed a thumb at the door.

"This is where, if you would, Jake, you can do me a favor," confided Bascom, leaning forward in the chair. "Kacey and I haven't been very damned close for a lot of years. I'm never going to agree with her politically, since she's a wild-eyed nut in that sphere. I would, though, like to see her more often than I do. After this mess is over . . . well, I'd like to stay in touch. This family crisis has brought her back into my circle and I'd like her to stay a mite closer from here on."

"She wants me to involve her in the investigation."

Bascom rubbed his hands, slowly, together. "I don't think Kacey ought to become deeply mixed up in this business," he said.

"But you don't want her to feel she's left out, either."

"That's about it. I'd be much obliged if you'd keep her distracted but not unhappy."

"Don't they ask goats to do this when they want to catch tigers?"

Bascom smiled. "You're very good at dealing with wacky women, Jake," he told his operative. "Roy Anselmo can't cope with Kacey if she starts poking around at the agency."

Jake said, "I'll give it a try."

7 • WHEN

the big robot rubbed his copper-plated hands together, they produced an echoing rasping sound. "This is swell, kids," he said in his deep rattling voice. "We just installed this dingus and it's supposed to be hot stuff. Unlike other identity imagers, this baby can—"

"Hey, we've got a class to get to in about sixteen minutes, Rex," said Dan, impatient.

Rex/GK-30 chuckled. "You flesh-and-blood types worry too much about a few unimportant minutes. If you look at time from a non-human perspective, why—"

"We are on sort of a tight schedule," added Molly. "We hoped just to pop in and out of Background & ID, consult you, and depart."

The robot, who was in charge of this sector of the SoCal Police Academy's information center, invited, "What say we get rolling, then?"

"I'll give you the descriptions I got from my friend, Rex, and you see what you can do. Okay?"

"Not necessary with this new, improved imager, kiddo." Rex pointed a large metallic forefinger at the small holostage that rested on the table in front of him. "Just speak the details. It'll do the rest."

Molly, nodding and clearing her throat, took a few steps closer to the table. She began by reciting the details that Susan Grossman had given her about the short red-haired man whom she'd seen in her vision when her brother had been killed.

When Molly concluded, the coppery robot requested of the gadget, "Let's see a visual, chum."

On the platform a doll-size image popped into being. It was a three-dimensional projection of an undersized red-headed man.

"That the gink?" asked Rex/GK-30.

"I never actually saw him," reminded Molly. "But Sue gave me fairly detailed descriptions of both the—"

"Perhaps we ought," suggested the robot, "to sneak this Sue frail in here so she can get a firsthand look-see."

"She's not able to leave home right now."

"Prostrated with grief, huh?"

Dan said, "No, too loony to be allowed to run around loose."

"We could vidphone her," offered Rex. "I can transmit this image over the—"

"That's not possible, either," put in Molly. "But why don't we get a tentative identification of people who fit this description? Then maybe I can show the photos to her."

"Possible makes," the robot told the projection device.

All at once a shrill bleating sound came from the voxbox at the base of the ID stage.

The image of the possible killer faded, to be replaced by the figure of a very similar red-haired man. But this time he was stretched out, naked, on a white metal table with a gray plyosheet half covering him.

"Salten, Leroy M.," droned the voxbox. "Matches prior simulation in seventeen of twenty ID points."

"Details on this stiff," urged the big copper-plated robot.

The metallic voice continued, "Leroy M. Salten was found at 6:14 this morning beneath Fun Pier 12 in the Long Beach Sector of Greater Los Angeles. He had been shot twice in the back with a standard lazgun. It is estimated that Salten had been dead for approximately two hours. Do you require a printed copy of his criminal record?"

"Yep," answered Rex. "And some pix."

"Alive or dead?"

"Both."

Dan touched Molly's hand. "Now I'm wondering."

"About what?" she asked.

He indicated the image of the dead man. "Your friend Sue Grossman thought she saw a mystical vision of a fellow who looked a lot like the guy that killed her brother," he said slowly. "And then—what? About four or so hours after that this same fellow is knocked off over in the Long Beach Sector. Logic tells me she couldn't have seen a picture of this guy in her head, but I don't know how else to explain it."

"Leroy Salten has to be one of the two men Sue saw in her vision," said Molly, convinced. "There's simply no other way she could've known about him."

"Coincidence?" offered the robot.

"Hooey," replied Molly.

"Hoax?"

"Nuts."

Dan, frowning, shook his head. "The trouble is, I don't believe in telepathy."

"You're," advised Molly, "going to have to change your notions."

Rex lumbered over to collect the report on the late Leroy Salten that had just come clicking out of the printer next to the ID stage. "Now, what about the other lug the little lady saw? Shall we try to get a make on him, kids?"

Molly said, "Yes, of course. Let's give him a try."

This time, however, they had no luck. The hairless man couldn't be identified at all.

JAKE ASKED his partner, "What meal is this you're indulging in?"

Looking up from his plate of soycakes and prosub, Gomez answered, "Late breakfast."

Tapping his finger against the side of his mug of nearcaf, Jake said, "At two in the afternoon?"

"It's too early for high tea and I'm skipping lunch all week as part of my new diet regimen." He patted his midsection a few times before turning to gaze out the plastiglass window of the diner toward the nearby afternoon Pacific. "How's our esteemed *comandante*?"

"Pissed off but otherwise in fine fettle. Hopes to be out and about no later than—"

"Once again," came a loud matronly voice from out of the half dozen voxboxes hanging up under the low neowood ceiling of the small seaside diner, "let us welcome you to Mom's, one of 864 friendly, homelike eating establishments in Greater Los Angeles. Remember, when it comes to home cooking and low, low prices, nobody beats Mom. Today's special is soycakes and prosub with sudaspuds on the side. Enjoy."

"Nice to know I'm in the culinary mainstream." Gomez forked up another bite of prosub.

Jake said, "I called the asshole and informed him that—"

"Meaning Roy Anselmo?"

"That asshole, yeah. I told him I want to do some digging into the life and times of Dwight Grossman," continued Jake. "Grossman worked for an outfit that researches companies for investors. His specialty was apparently pharmaceutical outfits."

"Doesn't sound like an especially hazardous profession."

"Depends on what you dig up," said Jake. "I'm also interested in Grossman's romantic life."

"Meaning he may have been annoying and bedeviling other ladies besides Kay Norwood?"

"Right, and perhaps somebody decided to curtail his harassing in a drastic way."

After wiping his mustache with a checkered plyonapkin, Gomez said, "Keep in mind, *amigo*, that we're dealing with folks who can do some pretty fancy technical fudging. Two separate"— he held up his forefinger and middle finger side by side— "security tapes show Bascom doing stuff we know he never did."

"I assume you're going to locate any experts hereabouts who are capable of that degree of electronic fakery?"

"*Sí*, of course," answered his partner. "I calculate there aren't

more than four, maybe five *pendejos* who do work good enough to
fool the SoCal constabulary *and* our own Doc Olan."

"We better split, then, Sid. I'll follow the Grossman angle, you
concentrate on who rigged the frame."

Gomez drank most of his citrisub juice. "You are looking, even
for the dour sourpuss you are, exceptionally downhearted this
afternoon, *compañero,*" he observed. "You holding back some
bad news?"

Jake looked out toward the hazy ocean. "Turns out I have an
honorary partner to contend with, Sid."

Gomez blinked. "*Ai,* surely nobody can replace me?"

"Kacey Bascom has volunteered her services to help save her
pop."

After exhaling a long, rueful sigh, Gomez said, "She's a very
pretty *mujer.* A few pounds too skinny for my tastes, yet I can
appreciate her general attractiveness." He sighed further. "Pity
she's politically only about two steps removed from the sort of
cabrones who'd like to see lovable liberal Latinos like me burned
at the stake."

"She happens to be working for Bracken just now."

"J. J. Bracken? The gent who makes Ebenezer Scrooge look
like a soft touch?"

"The esteemed star of *Facin' Bracken* himself. When she's not
doing research for his daily vidnet harangues, Kacey is going to
help me find out who really killed Grossman and why."

"What's the *jefe* say about that, Jake?"

"Hell, you know Bascom's never happy about his relationships
with his assorted offspring," answered Jake. "He's been pretty
much estranged from Kacey and he sees her coming to visit him
in the jug and offering to help as a wedge that—"

"Wedges are what Kacey's cronies like to drive through here-
tics' hearts," reminded his partner with a combination shrug and

shudder. "I thank the fates, *amigo,* that I'm too disreputable to be allowed anywhere near the formidable *Señorita* Kacey. How do you intend to handle this?"

"I'll try to humor the lady long as I can," said Jake. "If she gets too much underfoot, then I'll have to sideline her."

"Try not to break anything," cautioned Gomez.

8•SLOTz

is one of dozens of government-operated gambling parlors to be found in Greater Los Angeles. It's housed in a moderate-sized domed building in a hilly stretch of the Sherman Oaks Sector. There are no windows and only a minimum of interior light. Up to ninety patrons can use the compscreens to play simulated blackjack, slot machines, roulette, and 3D bingo. Nearly every player seat was filled that afternoon as Leo Anson walked through the dimlit circular room to halt in front of an opaque plasti-glass door.

The Cosmos Agency detective was a large man, dark, with short-cropped graying hair. He stood straight and still at the door, unmoving and uninterested in the electronic gaming going on all around him.

Just behind him, someone—sounded like an older woman—gave a pleased laugh and cried, "Bingo!"

Anson didn't turn around to look.

After rattling faintly, the door slid open.

The big detective hurried across the threshold. As the door shut quietly behind him, Anson was already hurrying down the ramp that led to the lower level of Slotz.

He stopped again in front of an opaque plastiglass door labeled PERSONNEL II.

After nearly thirty seconds that door slid open.

The room beyond was small and shadowy. A single compscreen sat glowing faintly on a three-legged green metal table at the cubicle's center.

Sitting in the straight green metal chair, Anson tapped the screen's control panel.

The screen presented an image of a sunlit field of wildflowers. A faint breeze was touching the blossoms and large white butterflies swirled and flickered in the afternoon air above the bright blossoms.

"You took your sweet time dragging your fat ass over here, Anson," observed the voxbox.

"I'm supposed to be working full-time on the Grossman case," reminded Anson.

"Work on the case, but get here when you're supposed to."

"I'm here now."

The metallic voice said, "Bascom's getting out."

"I hadn't heard that."

"He's being sprung by that lawyer broad. He'll be free before nightfall, looks like."

"You knew he had a hell of a lot of influence in Greater LA," said Anson. "So does Kay Norwood."

"We'd prefer him to stay inside longer and not get directly involved in this."

"Looks like that isn't going to happen, doesn't it?"

The voxbox asked, "What's Jake Cardigan up to?"

"He told Anselmo—you know, the guy who's temporarily in charge of Cosmos—he wanted to concentrate on Grossman, on his work, and his social life."

"Shit. Cardigan can be a pain in the butt."

"Quite often," agreed the detective.

"And what angle are you supposed to be working on?"

"The Grossman family so far. His father, his sister, and Juneanne Stackpoole, the current lady in the old boy's life."

"Do they know anything?"

"They don't seem to," said Anson. "But . . ."

"But what, asshole?"

"I'm still looking into something concerning the sister, Susan Grossman."

"She's a Tekhead, isn't she?"

"Used to be. She took a cure."

The voxbox laughed. "There's no cure."

"Cardigan's cured, too."

"Naw, they all come back. But get on about this sister of Grossman's."

"She made a couple of calls last night," Anson went on. "The first one to her brother at about a half hour after your people—"

"She couldn't have known a damn thing."

"Maybe, probably," Anson said. "Her second call was to a girl named Molly Fine."

"Who the hell is she?"

"Well, it happens I knew the answer to that without looking it up," said Anson. "Molly Fine attends the SoCal Police Academy and her steady beau is a boy named Dan Cardigan."

"Christ, Cardigan's kid."

"Cardigan's only kid, right."

"But Grossman's sister can't know a damn thing," insisted the voice.

"Can't she?"

After a few seconds: "Find out what she does know, Anson. And check up on this Molly Fine. I don't like her being chummy with Cardigan's boy."

Anson said, "That's going to involve extra money."

"Bullshit, we're already paying you a hefty—"

"I may have to get close to Jake Cardigan," pointed out the operative. "That wasn't part of our original deal."

"$5,000 on top of what you're already getting."

"Has to be $10,000."

"We can't go higher than $5,000."

Anson said, "I'll settle for that. For now anyway."

There was a whirring, and a yellow chit came easing out of a thin slot in the voxbox. "Congratulations. You just won five thousand bucks at roulette. Take this upstairs and cash it in."

GOMEZ CEASED WHISTLING.

The immense warehouse he'd stepped into out of the afternoon was chill and musty. The beams of thin sunlight slanting down across it were spotted with flecks of drifting black dust. Lined up in the gloom were rows of immobile androids. Those standing stiffly on the right-hand side of the Pasadena Sector storehouse were butler androids; those on the left, maids and cooks.

The curly-haired detective moved deeper into the murky interior. *"Buenos días,"* he said loudly.

At the far end of the warehouse was a rickety worktable. A partially dismantled butler lay outstretched atop the table and a thin pale man in a gray smock was hunched over it and tinkering. "Don't get too close, Sidney," he warned in a hoarse voice. "This may be contagious."

"Another malady, Pegler?"

Pegler sneezed twice. Then once again. "I'm pretty near certain of the cause," he said, sniffling. "It's a conspiracy and I've got the suspects narrowed down to two or possibly three of my former wives."

"What is it you think you're suffering from?"

"It's called a cold." He sniffled again, dabbing at his nose with a plyochief.

"Nobody gets colds anymore." Gomez eased closer. "Not since the vaccine came into use thirty years ago. Don't you get your shots every—"

"This is bacteriological warfare stuff." Pegler set aside the electric screwdriver he was using on the android butler's interior workings.

"Your wives are practicing biological warfare?"

"They, most of them, get very upset when I leave them. Some of the more vindictive ones have cooked up this scheme. I'm near certain." He sneezed again.

"Are you," inquired Gomez, "well enough to do some business?"

Pegler blew his nose. "If it weren't for my sideline as a first-rate informant, Sidney, I'd waste away. Nobody wants to rent butlers anymore. Especially not these upper-crust traditional British models." He tapped the andy he was working on, then gestured at the rows of maids. "We still get a few calls for the French maids, but mostly from people who want them for immoral purposes."

Gomez nodded sympathetically, then said, "If I wanted to tamper with a security tape, fake something so effectively that it would fool not only the law but *hombres* with laminated diplomas from the crackerjack forensic institutions of—"

"I can't help you, Sidney." Pegler held up his right hand in a stop-right-there gesture.

"*¿Qué pasa?* I haven't even outlined my inquiry and you—"

"This is the Bascom business." Pegler sneezed twice more. "No, not safe."

"Whoa now. Has somebody warned you to stay away from this?"

"You better try somebody else," advised the frail man in a whisper. "But me, I can't—oh, shit!" Eyes going wide, he was looking behind and beyond the detective.

Gomez turned and saw two large butlers, each carrying a lazgun, striding in his direction.

9 ● THE

large, pale man sitting on the green metal park bench had absolutely no hair, not so much as an eyebrow. He was, with big dead-white hands folded in his lap, watching a tiny robot canary that was perched on a branch of a simulated oak nearby. A thin smile touched his colorless lips.

Jake was moving along a wide path that led through the holographic park to the cluster of cottages that housed Thelwell Brokerage Services.

"Excuse me, sir," said the hairless man in a high-pitched voice as Jake neared the bench.

Jake slowed. "Yeah?"

"What might your business be?"

Jake stopped. "Might that be any of your damned business?"

Smiling another small smile, the big man rose up. He was a few inches taller than Jake. "As a matter of fact, sir, it is," he replied in his piping voice. "I handle security for Thelwell, and any and all unauthorized visitors to the facility have to—"

"I got authorization over the phone couple hours ago." Jake started to move on.

He put a hand on Jake's arm. "You're not on my list, sir."

"That doesn't actually upset me all that much. Now, let go of—"

"I'm really afraid I have to see your identification, sir, or I'll be forced to—*oof!*"

Jake's left fist had delivered two swift and hard punches to the hairless man's midsection.

The man wobbled, began to sink. But he still tried to tug a weapon out of his shoulder holster.

Jake hopped back, booting him in the chin.

Sighing a high-pitched sigh, the big man sprawled out on the simulated moss.

Crouching, Jake eased out the gun the security man had been reaching for. "A lazgun," he reflected, sliding it into his jacket pocket. "These folks are damn serious about security."

Leaving the unconscious man sprawled where he'd dropped, Jake continued along the path to the cottage complex.

The Reception cottage, like the dozen others, was designed to look as though it were made of stucco and timbers. The windows were imitation stained glass and the sharply slanting roof appeared to be of bright yellow straw.

In the cozy parlor Jake told the pretty blond android at the desk, "You better go take a look at your security lout. He seems to have swooned."

"Beg pardon?" The mechanical young woman pushed back from her desk.

"Big lunk with a scarcity of hair," amplified Jake, pointing at the doorway with his thumb. "Passed out up the garden path there."

Puzzled, the blond andy shook her head. "All our security is electronic," she said. "We don't have any actual guards, human or robotic."

Spinning on his heel, Jake ran out of the cozy cottage and back along the woodland path.

But when he reached the spot where he'd had his dispute, the hairless man was not there.

"I'VE ALWAYS HAD a great deal of respect for the Cosmos outfit," announced Edmond Flenniker, a short, chunky man in his middle thirties. "I'm sorry you got roughed up while visiting us here at Thelwell, but I assure you I have no idea who that hooligan was or—Maggie, what did I say about this sandwich?"

"Something rude and lowbrow as I recall," replied the black woman sitting in one of the chairs facing the Thelwell Brokerage Services president's wide, silvery desk.

Flenniker grabbed a plazplate up off the desk and pointed an accusing finger at the sandwich resting upon it. "Is this curried soyloaf, Maggie darling?"

"Sure looks like it to me. Smells like it, too."

"What's your opinion, Cardigan?" He thrust the plate toward Jake, who was in a rubberoid chair just to the left of the glistening desk.

"Fits the description."

"It's curried lentil loaf if it's anything. I have a highly overpaid executive secretary, Maggie darling, so that when I send out for a curried soyloaf sandwich on Siberian plowboy black bread, that is what is brought back to—mother of God, this isn't even Siberian plowboy black bread." When he slapped the plate back on the desktop, the sandwich hopped twice. "Maggie, what am I to do with you?"

"Fire me and pay me that huge severance bonus," suggested Maggie Sleet, crossing her legs.

Hunkering down in his chair, the Thelwell president said, "There are no avocado chips, either."

"You already ate them."

"When did I do that?"

"Recently."

"Didn't I ask you to get a double order of chips?"

"Nope."

Flenniker sat silent for a while and concentrated on breathing in and out. Eventually he spoke. "I don't want to let these little staff problems interfere with my helping you out, Cardigan. What is it you want to know about poor Dwight Grossman? Maggie, didn't I also request a papaya fruitzer?"

"In the cup there." She pointed.

Grabbing up the indicated cup, he sniffed at it. "Mango or I'm a goof."

"Man said it was papaya."

"No use sending you back, Maggie darling, he'd only hoodwink you again." He took a very tentative sip. "Yike, it's gone rancid to boot."

Jake said, "Do you have any ideas about why someone would want to kill Grossman?"

"Someone, you mean, besides your insanely jealous and vindictive boss?"

"Walt Bascom didn't kill him."

"Ah, I like to see company loyalty. Maggie here would send me up the river in a trice."

"Half a trice," she corrected.

Flenniker grew thoughtful, wrinkles furrowed his brow. "Dwight was, far as I could tell, a rather bland guy. Very efficient, cooperative, but no fireball," he said finally. "He wasn't sensationally popular here at Thelwell, but nobody disliked him. He got along well with the rest of the gang."

"Yet he was threatening Kay Norwood, harassing her quite a bit."

"A side of his character I wasn't at all aware of."

"Talk to his wife," suggested Maggie, uncrossing her legs.

"I'm planning to. But what's your reason for suggesting it?"

"He gave her a very rough time after she left him, same kind of tricks I hear he used on the lawyer lady."

"Is this office gossip of any use to you, Cardigan?"

"At this point, anything may be useful."

The Thelwell executive said, "We've been preparing a series of reports on half a dozen pharmaceutical outfits in the Greater LA area, to help our clients make their investment decisions. Dwight was handling those."

"Did he report anything unusual to you? Mention having trouble with any of these companies?"

Flenniker shook his head. "Far as I know, he hadn't turned up anything unusual enough to mention."

"Can I see copies of those reports?"

Glancing at Maggie, the president asked, "Do we have them on file?"

"He hadn't turned anything in as yet."

Jake asked, "Did Grossman work by himself?"

"Yes, he was pretty much a loner," answered Flenniker.

"What about Hermione?" put in Maggie, crossing her legs again.

"Oh, I don't think she had very much to do with—"

"Who is she?" Jake asked them.

"Hermione Earnshaw," Maggie told him. "She was Grossman's assistant until last week."

"What is she now?"

"Gone," said Maggie.

"She left the firm," said Flenniker.

"Going where?"

"Personnel can tell you. Although I don't think she'll be any help."

"Going to be fun trying to find her," added Maggie.

Jake eyed her. "Meaning?"

"Hermione left her condo in the Riverside Sector. Nobody knows where she is now."

"Oh, I'm certain there are plenty of her friends who know where she's gotten to," said Flenniker. "Now, Maggie darling, if you're through gossiping, you might get Cardigan that list of companies poor Dwight was investigating."

Maggie stood up. "I'd find Hermione," she advised as she left the office.

10 •W

E want to persuade you, Gomez, old chap," explained one of the approaching large android butlers, brandishing his ebony lazgun.

"Dissuade you actually, old thing," added the other lumbering andy.

Gomez glanced back at Pegler and muttered, "Betrayed."

Cringing behind his worktable, the frail informant sneezed and said, "I'm a mere bystander, Sidney."

"I suspect, *cabrón*, that you . . ." Gomez gave a sudden gasp. He took a wobbly step to his left, two wobbly steps to his right.

"No rum behavior, old bean," warned one of the butlers as he came clunking closer.

"I fear it's . . . it's . . . *¡Dios!* One of my spells." Unexpectedly, Gomez dropped suddenly to the floor.

When he was flat out on his back, he went swiftly elbowing across the floorboards.

" 'Ere now, none of that!" One of the androids swung his lazgun around and fired.

The crackling beam ate a deep blackish rut in the neowood.

By that time Gomez was scooting under the worktable.

He popped to his feet, kicked out, and toppled the table.

The defunct android that had been reclining there hit the floor, spewing inner workings, and went rolling and rattling toward the charging butlers.

Diving to the floor again, but drawing out his stungun as he dropped, Gomez fired.

"Blimey!" exclaimed one of the androids when the beam of the stunner hit him full in his broad chest and disabled him.

He fell floorward and hit with an impressive hollow thunk.

The surviving butler tried a lazgun shot at Gomez, but only succeeded in slicing the table clean in half.

Gomez jumped upright once again and shot at the second would-be assailant.

The stunbeam went wide, hitting a plump cook android and knocking her off her perch.

Gomez's second shot did better, and the andy butler dropped his lazgun and then followed it to the floor.

Leaping over the sundered table, Gomez caught Pegler by the collar and yanked him out of the cringing crouch he had assumed. "Now, *perrito,* I'd be most grateful if you'd inform me, at no charge, who hired you to do me in?"

The shivering informant sneezed. "You really shouldn't get so close to me, Sidney, you're liable to catch my—"

"Who?"

"How's that?"

"Who arranged to have those mechanical louts assassinate me?"

Sniffling, Pegler replied, "It was, I swear, as big a surprise to me as it must have been to you when those lads came to life. I assumed they were dormant and—"

"Apparently, *tonto,* you are unfamiliar with the fabled Gomez intelligence." The angry detective commenced shaking the other man some. "*Sí,* each and every member of the Gomez clan is nowhere near stupid enough to believe this kind of bunk. *Por favor,* before I lose the saintly patience I am exhibiting at the moment, give me the truth." He shook the sniffling Pegler several more times.

"I swear I have absolutely no—"

"Usually, *pendejo,* I refrain from using a lazgun," said Gomez quietly and evenly. "However, I notice that there are two handsome such weapons lying about your establishment, dropped by the *cholos* you rigged to do me in. If you wouldn't like to have your nasal passages cleaned out by a lazbeam, now's the time to confide."

"I don't know who they were, truly."

"Details, *por favor.*"

"There was a vidphone call about midday, but the screen stayed blank and the voice was filtered." Pausing to sneeze, the informant continued. "I was instructed to fix a couple of my androids to throw a scare into you. In fact, Sidney, they suggested I rig four, but, being a pal of yours, I only—"

"They knew I was going to call on you, huh? But I didn't contact you in advance."

"My impression, for what it's worth, is that they contacted anybody who has knowledge about people who are expert at sec-system modifications."

"That's *muy* interesting, their knowing what I was going to be digging into today," reflected Gomez, letting the ailing informant go.

"I'd be extremely careful, Sidney, if you're planning to call on any of my colleagues for further info."

Stepping back, Gomez scrutinized the man. "Were they Tek hoods, Pegler?"

"I tell you, I don't know who they were. This voice offered me a fee—and, Sidney, he threatened to do me considerable harm if I didn't go along with it," said Pegler. "The andies, in spite of what you might think, weren't fixed to kill you. Only to scare you off."

"Oh, *sí*, I believe that," he said. "Scare me off what, did they tell you that?"

Pegler shook his head and then sneezed twice more. "Whatever you're working on. That was the message."

"I think it would be beneficial if you remained quiet and uncommunicative for the remainder of today."

"I will, Sidney. I'll close up shop and go to the beach down at—"

"No, you'll simply take a long nap." Pointing the stungun at him, Gomez squeezed the trigger.

U P   N E A R the high, curved ceiling of the immense AdVillage reception area a huge six-foot-tall green plazbottle of Bliss Kola tilted exactly every twenty-one seconds to send a foamy stream of brownish liquid cascading down fifteen feet to splash into the wide oval fountain at the center of the mosaic tile floor. Each projected tile represented a product label, and the hundreds of them made for a bright, gaudy spread.

Jake was sitting in one of the seven Lucite chairs in the row to the left of the boomerang-shaped reception desk. The six others sharing the bank of seats were all clad in medical garb, doctor smocks and nurse uniforms.

The portly gray-haired man next to Jake leaned and mentioned, "You should have dressed for the part."

"Hmm?"

"The casting android for the StanCo Pharmaceuticals account likes auditioning actors to show a bit of initiative and imagination," continued the man in the white coat. "Another friendly tip—you're a mite too weather-beaten to do a convincing physician."

"Think so?" asked Jake.

"I see you in tobaccosub spots, maybe booze and brainstim. That kind of muscular stuff," said the actor. "I don't know your work. What are your credits?"

Jake grinned. "Actually I'm not here to audition for anything," he said. "I'm waiting to see an agency art director."

"Not an actor, eh?"

"Nope."

"Odd, very odd. Because you have that mixture of cockiness and desperation that characterizes our profession."

"That could be because—"

"Mr. Cardigan?" said the voxbox embedded in the reception desk.

He stood up. "Yeah."

"Door G, please. That will lead you to the Persuasion, Ltd., wing of AdVillage."

Jake bowed toward the portly would-be physician, gave the desk a lazy salute, and headed for the designated doorway, striding across the multicolored imitation tiles.

.   .   .   .

MARGO LARIAR WAS an extremely blond woman in her middle thirties. Her attention was divided between Jake, whom she'd nodded onto a polka dot couch, and the six large compscreens on the wall facing her.

"Which color scheme up there makes you feel less anxious?" Dwight Grossman's former wife asked.

"I don't feel anxious."

"Well, hell, play along, Cardigan," she urged. "Assume you are, which, Jesus, most every other living soul in Greater LA is. Which of those rough-intrusion ads would soothe you?"

"When intrusion ads pop onto my vidwall or my compscreen, I merely get ticked off. There's not a one of them would soothe me," he answered. "Now, about the—"

"How about the one that's all blues?" Margo touched the keyboard that sat on her small white desk. "Or is this better now? You'll notice that I've subdued the shades of blue and added a—"

"You'll notice I'm standing over you, looking notably unsoothed."

She turned to face him. "Oh, I'm sorry as can be. I tend to get all tangled up in my work and ignore the—excuse me." Her fingers went flickering over the keyboard again. "But there. Doesn't that number-five layout have increased appeal now with more yellow in it?" She nodded to herself. "Where was I? Oh, yes, how can I help you, Cardigan?"

He nodded at her desk. "Suppose you switch to the sofa and I sit here?"

"Well, I feel uneasy when I'm not in my familiar—"

"Maybe you can use some—what the hell is it called?" He looked over at the rough ad layouts on the wall. "Yeah, some Kalmz."

"Oh, hell, I'd never take that swill." Slowly, a bit reluctantly, she left her desk to move to the polka dot couch.

Jake began, "First off, I don't believe Walt Bascom killed your husband. So can—"

"*Former* husband, *erstwhile* spouse," she quickly corrected. "I'm Margo Lariar now."

"And you felt well rid of the guy?"

Margo smiled, nodding. "Dwight was an extremely unsatisfactory man. He was violent, possessive, fastidious beyond belief. And he loved to do those dreadful company reports of his, to burrow into all sorts of places he shouldn't even have been, to bribe information out of—"

"We'll get to those reports," cut in Jake. "I take it you left him?"

"You bet your ass I did, yessir." She swung her right hand rapidly through the air. "Fast as I could."

"Did he harass you after that?"

"Absolutely. Vidphone calls—some pleading, most of them threatening. He'd attempt to break in to my place, he'd confront me in public places," said the former Mrs. Grossman. "Finally I put the law on Dwight and he subsided. A great many bullies are chickenshit underneath. Have you noticed?"

Jake said, "He was doing all those tricks with Kay Norwood."

"And others, believe me."

"At the same time?"

"Oh, no, Dwight was a one-woman psycho. Poor Kay Norwood was simply the latest target for his unrequited passion. Jesus, what a schmuck he was—rest his soul."

Jake said, "You're suggesting there might be a whole batch of women who didn't have much love for him?"

"Seven or eight at least that dear Dwight plagued, yes."

"Can you provide a list?"

"A partial one probably. I didn't keep up with his activities, but I heard things now and then."

"Grossman was doing research on several SoCal pharmaceutical outfits," continued Jake, straddling her desk chair. "One of them happened to be StanCo. Does your agency handle that account?"

She pointed at the far wall. "No, that's Alch & Associates, one of our neighbors here in AdVillage."

"While he was doing these reports, did he contact you for any—"

"Dwight couldn't contact me for any reason," she put in. "I never allowed him to communicate with me in any way," replied Margo, her attention partially straying to the rough layouts on the wall. "Although I did hear something about this pharmaceutical project of his just recently."

"What?"

"Only that—and this came from a friend of a friend after they heard he'd been killed—only that Dwight had seemed extremely uneasy the last days before he died. I have no idea of the reason."

"Who was the source of this news?"

She shook her head. "I'll have to see if she wants to be part of your investigation, Cardigan."

"Okay," he said. "Do you know Hermione Earnshaw?"

"Not as well as dear departed Dwight did," she replied, laughing. "Hermione was his loyal assistant at Thelwell and, I'm fairly certain, frequent bedmate. In spite of their political differences, they remained extremely chummy and Dwight never apparently threatened her. That was because, if you want my opinion, little skinny Hermione did a hell of a lot of the work that Dwight took the credit for."

"She seems to have dropped from sight."

"Maybe she joined a convent and went into mourning."

Jake said, "Tell me about their political differences."

"Hermione's very—excessively, make that—conservative,"

Margo answered. "She's a very active member of that nutcake group J. J. Bracken supports so enthusiastically. The Pure California Coalition. Christ, what a state this is." She started to get up, reconsidered and sat, then hopped to her feet. "I really have to get back to work. But, I swear to God, I'll send you that list of the other unfortunate ladies whose lives were blighted by Dwight since we split up."

Jake studied the six compscreens again before heading for the way out. "I'd go with the blue," he advised.

11 • GOMEz

adjusted his big red nose and went, huge yellow shoes flapping, hurrying into the seventeenth level of a Westwood Sector building. Just across the threshold, he set down a sample case that had BUFFOON ELECTRONIC TOYS, INC. emblazoned on its bright green side.

"Pipe the getup on this dodo," commented a little golden-haired doll that rested on a low ivory pedestal.

"A rube from Hicksville if ever I saw one," added a large robot rag doll who was slumped in a little plaz rocking chair.

A two-foot-high mechanical cowboy whipped off his Stetson. "Don't let them impolite bimbos a-rile ya, pardner," he drawled. "What kin I do ya fer?"

"Is the lady of the house in?" Gomez scratched at his frizzy purple wig.

The golden-haired blond doll suggested, "Why don't you take a hike, Zeke?"

"Yeah," seconded the rag doll, thumbing her nose in a floppy manner, "hit the road, bozo."

"Little dears, for shame." A fat silver-haired woman in a flowered tent dress had come jiggling out of the back office of the toy shop. "Is this any way to treat a respected customer?"

"This doink's not a paying customer, Corky," said the rag doll disdainfully. "He's just a schlep of a salesman."

Clearing his throat, Gomez said, "*Chiquita,* I have to communicate with you, *muy pronto.* For the usual fee, be it understood."

Blinking, Corky Keepnews took a jiggling step back. "Holy crow, is that you, Gomez honey?"

"*Sí,* but cleverly disguised so as not to tip off the opposition."

"Wow, it's not especially safe for you to be seen in the open."

"Hence the mummery, *bonita.*" He went flat-footing after her into her office.

Bidding the door to shut, Corky seated herself in an ample armchair. "I can't chat with you for more than five minutes, hon," she warned him.

From the one narrow viewindow you could see part of University of SoCal Campus 26, where either a riot or a rally was in progress in the Glade. "Why, in this instance, do I find myself on the shit list?" Gomez inquired. "Any hints?"

Corky narrowed her left eye and scrutinized the pale pink ceiling above her. "Somebody powerful is annoyed with you."

"Details?"

"I hear Teklords. One Teklord actually."

"Who?" He sat on the edge of the armchair opposite her and made a give-me-more-details motion with both yellow-gloved hands.

When Corky shook her head, her silver-blond hair flickered and danced. "I've got no details, Gomez. Don't, if you want the absolute truth, want any more than I got. But it's a very powerful gent."

"There are any number of Tek industrialists who fit that description. Can you zero in some, Cork?"

"West Coast, probably. As close as I can get, honey."

"Has it got to do with the Dwight Grossman kill?"

Giving the pink ceiling her attention again, the information dealer answered, "So they say."

"How the devil was Grossman connected to the Tek trade, Corky?"

"That I have no idea about." She lowered her husky voice. "Way I hear it, this poor sappo Grossman found out something he *really* wasn't supposed to know."

"And they want to eradicate me before I find out the same darn thing?"

"It's not certain, sweet, that they want you completely and totally dead," she informed him. "Might be they just mean to incapacitate you for a good while."

Gomez stroked his clown nose. "What about the Bascom frame-up?"

"Same bunch is behind that."

"I'm trying to find out who faked the security camera tapes," he told her. "But my usual experts at providing that sort of information have been alerted to booby-trap, sabotage, and otherwise futz me up. Who else besides the usual gang can I get what I need from?"

Corky's voice dropped even lower. "You might try a guy who does business as Einstein, Inc. Out in the Woodland Hills Sector of Greater LA."

"Never heard of the *hombre.*"

"Neither have the Teklords. Yet," Corky said. "You better talk to him before they get wind."

Rising, Gomez said, "*Gracias,* dear lady. How much do I owe you?"

"On the house, honey," she told him.

"*¿Por que?*"

"A going-away present."

"I'm not going away."

"But you ought to," Corky advised as he took his leave.

J. J. BRACKEN bounced twice in his high-back black metal chair, jabbed a finger in the direction of the empty chair facing him, and laughed. A lock of his pale blond hair fell down across his smooth forehead. He brushed it back, laughed again. "It appears, appears, cousins, that my Hotseat guest for tonight, yes, tonight's vidnet broadcast of your favorite, and mine, that's for sure, *Facin' Bracken,* is too yellow, yellow and chickenhearted, I'd say, wouldn't you, to show up." He clapped his hands together several times. "Or could it be, you think maybe, that the old girl came to what senses, senses, she has left and decided, as I've long maintained about her and the nattering nitwits who follow her, that it's time to throw in the towel, right, the towel."

A faint shimmering commenced in the vicinity of the other black chair.

Bouncing again, Bracken made a chuckling sound and brushed back the lock of unruly hair again. "Hush, cousins, somebody's coming."

Gradually, with some electrical sputtering and a few flashes of greenish light, the holographic image of a lean, gray-haired woman of seventy-five appeared in the guest chair.

Bracken hunched, watching the newly materialized projection.

"It appears, cousins, that she didn't do the smart thing and visit a suicide clinic," he said. "No, she decided to brazen it out and actually face me on my, popular, as you well know, my popular *Facin' Bracken* broadcast for tonight. Well, this is going to be, if the old darling can survive the heat, an interesting little—"

"Let me point out, Mr. Bracken," said the image of his guest, "that my delay in arriving was caused entirely by the clumsy and inept technicians you sent to my home to—"

"Quit whining, dear," interrupted the host. "Let me introduce you, will you? Cousins, this is none other than the notorious old-ster, Dr. Audrey Eisenberg, right, Eisenberg, a, I believe, Jewish name, but that doesn't bother us, cousins, does it? Dr. Eisenberg, who's not a medical doctor, not even one of these quacks who believes in keeping doddering wrecks alive once they've ceased to have any value to us in normal society, she's not a medical person but only a doctor of philosophy. We all are philosophers, aren't we, cousins? You don't need a lot of high-blown school-ing for that, high-blown and expensive. Most of you know, cousins, that the doctor here, the nice Jewish doctor, believes that we ought to let oldsters just go on living, year after year, and drain our coffers, instead of climbing into their coffins as they ought or—"

"As I suspected, Mr. Bracken, you intend to indulge in one of your usual windy harangues and not allow me to—"

"Let's start with the Bible, Doc," he said. "Apparently you don't agree that three score and ten years is all we ought to have. You, as I think you're saying in your various lectures to fellow oldsters . . ."

Up in the engineer's booth, Kacey Bascom was sitting and watching her boss. She looked up from the copy of his notes for tonight's broadcast and made a signal to him. It was a small gesture that meant she thought he was being too rough too soon with the elderly guest. "Pull back a bit," she mouthed.

Bracken caught her warning, but gave a quick negative shake of his head.

Both the technicians sharing the booth with the young woman were robots. The chrome-plated one said to her, "What's his stand on old robots?"

"This is a serious issue, Jocko, not something to kid about," Kacey responded. "The number of useless oldsters in SoCal is increasing at an alarming rate and unless something—"

"Too bad they don't have scrap yards for people," said Jocko, returning his attention to the control panel.

"I'm here to cooperate and work side by side," said a voice behind her.

Kacey turned in time to see the rear door easing shut. Jake was in the small room with her and the robots. "How the hell did you get up here? The studio has security people on every entrance to keep out fanatics and people who might have a grudge against J.J."

"Apparently I don't look like a fanatic." Jake came over to take the empty chair next to hers. "They let me right on in."

"No, no one without authorization and proper ID is allowed on this level of the facility, Jake."

"Most of the security people I encountered were flat on their ass and unconscious," he explained. "So nobody asked for any identification. If I'm someplace I'm not supposed to be, why, I'll—"

"What did you do, use bullying private-cop tricks to force your way—"

"There's something you may be able to help me on, Kacey."

She glanced down at J. J. Bracken, who was pointing at Dr.

Eisenberg and saying, "But if you people all died at seventy, think of the savings it would mean to . . ."

Kacey asked Jake, "This is about my father?"

"It's not about my plans for eliminating old age from SoCal," he answered. "Can we talk somewhere?"

Kacey frowned, then gave Bracken another signal. "Jocko, I'm going out for a bit."

"Sure, gather rosebuds while you may," the robot advised.

"I wonder who built all that sort of poetic nonsense into you."

"Nobody. I do a lot of reading on my own."

Taking Jake's arm, she led him toward the doorway. "We'll use the staff exit so not too many security people will notice you."

Jake grinned. "Most of them will be snoozing for a while yet," he said.

12 ● GOMEz

thrust a booted foot out and prevented the proprietor of Einstein, Inc., from shutting the door. *"Momentito,"* he requested, shouldering the plastiglass door and forcing the small, balding man back inside the narrow shop. "I'm interested in conversing with you, *señor.*"

"I'm closing," said the small man as he backed away from the intruder. "In fact, I'm closing down for an indefinite period. I'm going on an extended leave." He bumped into one of the two large suitcases sitting on the floor and started to fall.

Catching him and uprighting him, Gomez said, "Corky Keepnews suggested that you—"

"Oh, Lord. I'm too late."

Three of the small, neat shop's walls had wide shelves that contained what was labeled as either ANTIQUE SOFTWARE or VINTAGE
COMPUTERS.

"I'm with the Cosmos Detective Agency," explained Gomez as
he placed the nervous man in a straight-backed chair.

"So you say."

"You're the owner here?"

"Probably."

"Why do you call the business Einstein, Inc.?"

"Because I'm Einstein. Milton Einstein." Leaving the chair, he
made a grab for one of his suitcases. "You'll excuse me, but I'm
on my way to . . . well, let's just say elsewhere."

Gomez booted the suitcase out of his reach. "Corky tells me
your specialty is providing information about technically skilled
hombres who do illicit futzing with vidtapes and—"

"She's behind the times," put in Einstein, edging toward his
other suitcase. "I was *formerly* in that sideline. But I've retired."

"Do you know who faked the Bascom tapes?"

"I used to know," admitted Einstein as he bent to take hold of
the suitcase handle. "Too bad you didn't get here earlier, before I
went out of business."

"Tell me, Einstein." He took the suitcase away from him.

"I started hearing some terrible things a few hours ago and I've
decided it isn't safe to continue—"

"That's what informants are supposed to do, Einstein, hear terrible things," reminded Gomez. "Then they pass such stuff on and
collect rich rewards and—"

"No, there are Tek people involved, high-up Tek people. The
kind who think nothing of having upstart information peddlers
terminated."

"My name is Gomez. Call Corky, would you?" suggested the

detective. "She'll, I assure you, point out that I tend to do great harm to folks who don't comply with my search for enlightenment." He smiled. "Who did the job on those tapes?"

"I'm late for my skyliner. I have to go, Gomez."

"You'll never go anywhere, Einstein, unless you confide."

He glanced fretfully from one suitcase to the other. "It's a shame I ever decided to go into this end of the information business," he lamented.

"After you fill me in, I'll put you in touch with a first-rate crackerjack career counselor." Gomez got a firm grip on the man's arm. "Give me the fellow's name, *por favor.*"

Einstein swallowed, coughed, swallowed again. "It was Avram Moyech."

"I thought Moyech was a SoCal Tech professor who worked undercover for the Greater LA branch of the Office of Clandestine Operations."

"Avram quit that when he retired from SoCal Tech. Went into business for himself about five months ago."

"Where is he at this moment?"

Einstein coughed again. "Out of town."

"Where did he go?"

"Texas. All I know is he went to Texas a couple days ago."

"Texas is *muy grande.* Give me a location."

"Sweetwater, Texas. Around Sweetwater someplace. That's all I know, really, Gomez."

Gomez said, "Now, how about the *cabrones* who hired Moyech for the task?"

"I don't know that, don't have details." Einstein looked uneasily toward the doorway. "It's obviously a big Tek cartel, but I don't know which one."

"Why'd they kill Dwight Grossman?"

"For good and sufficient reasons, but reasons, Gomez, that are unknown to me. I have to go now."

"Can I help carry your bags to your skycar?" offered the detective.

"No, no, thanks." Einstein shook his head. "I'd prefer not to be seen with you out in the open."

"*Gracias,* then." Gomez left the shop.

"FREE," said Bascom, "more or less." He was sitting in the passenger seat of a skycar that was speeding through the twilight sky of Greater LA, away from jail and toward home. "I appreciate your efforts, Kay."

Kay Norwood, a tall blond woman, was in the pilot seat. "They really had you embedded deeply in the lockup, Walt," she said. "I had to pull considerable strings to extract you. And you're still going to have to stand trial."

"Nope, they're never going to try me for the Grossman killing."

"Because you and your Cosmos Detective Agency are going to find the real murderer?"

The chief of Cosmos nodded, smiling thinly. "That's exactly what's going to happen," he assured her.

"So far nobody thinks those tapes aren't authentic, including your own experts."

"We *know* the damn things were rigged, so eventually we'll prove it," he said confidently. "Now, give me some more background on Dwight Grossman."

"I only went out with him seven or eight times over a stretch of two or three months. But it didn't take much to get the guy fixated, I guess," the attorney answered.

Below them, as the night closed in, more and more lights were blossoming across Greater Los Angeles.

"What he tried on you, the harassing and the threats, he must've done to other ladies as well."

"I assume so, Walt, but I don't know who any of his other targets might have been."

"That's okay, Cardigan will get that information," he said. "What about Grossman's work? Would the fact-finding missions he undertook for Thelwell have given somebody a reason to knock him off?"

Kay started to shake her head. Then said, "Well, actually, I'm not certain."

He put his hand over hers. "You remembered something, Kay?"

"Only something he said one of the last times he made a vidphone call to me," she said. "He bragged, in between threats, that he was going to be very rich soon and then maybe I'd be sorry for dropping him. All his years as an investigator were going to pay off."

"Blackmail maybe?"

"That could have been what Dwight had in mind," she acknowledged. "The thing is, Walt, he was a braggart much of the time, and that may have been merely a lie to impress me."

"Suppose it wasn't—any notion where this money was going to come from?"

"I think he implied it had something to do with the reports he was working on at the moment."

"Then we—"

"You ought to see this, Bascom," suddenly said the voxbox beneath the dash panel phonescreen.

"What the hell is going on?" The agency chief scowled at the now-glowing screen.

The image of a bright afternoon living room appeared. The room was white and pale blue, and outside its high, wide windows, gulls could be seen diving toward a patch of ocean.

"That's my place," realized Kay, inhaling sharply. "And that's me."

The blond attorney was crossing the room, moving toward the windows. She stopped, turned abruptly, and said, "What's wrong, Walt? Why are you here?"

"You were still sleeping with that bastard, weren't you?" Bascom, in a rumpled suit, was stomping closer to the obviously frightened woman. "I killed him and then it turns out you were lovers."

"Get out, Walt," she demanded. "I don't want you around when you're in one of these violent, angry moods!"

"Bullshit! We're going to settle this, Kay," he shouted at her. "You lied to me all along. You were sleeping with him and telling me you didn't want him bothering you."

"That's not true. Now get out or—"

"Bitch. Lying, unfaithful bitch!" Bascom had yanked out a lazgun. He made a snarling sound and fired at Kay.

As the beam burned deep into her chest the picture faded from the screen.

"Thought you might like a glimpse of the future," said the voxbox.

13 • THE

jungle was eleven levels below the ground, under the Glendale Sector of Greater Los Angeles. It went stretching away for several acres beyond the elevator exit. A perpetual sunlight illuminated the sky above the intricate tangle of trees, leaves, fronds, vines, and flowers.

Kacey put a restraining hand on Jake's arm, saying quietly, "I'll handle all the encounters down here."

"Fine."

Two green-uniformed young men, large and thick, were trotting toward them along the simulated jungle trail. Each carried a lazrifle.

Kacey told the Pure California Coalition sentries, "We have a pass from Colonel Burns."

The thicker of the pair held out his hand. "See it."

She produced a small plaz rectangle from her slax pocket. "We have permission to—"

"See it," repeated the sentry.

She placed it on his open palm.

"Looks up-and-up." He handed it to his colleague.

"Looks up-and-up."

"We have permission to visit Hermione Earnshaw," Kacey explained.

"What it says," agreed the first sentry, retrieving the pass from the second sentry and returning it to the young woman.

"Thanks," she said. "We'll continue on our way, then."

The first sentry was scrutinizing Jake. "What are you?"

"Beg pardon?"

"Got a race card?"

Kacey stepped in front of Jake. "Neither of us has one. Colonel Burns will vouch for—"

"You a Mex?" the sentry asked Jake, moving Kacey aside with the flat of his hand.

Jake grinned. "I'm not, but if I were I don't see that it's the business of a dim-witted lunk who's playing soldier in a make-believe jungle eleven levels under, of all places, the goddamn Glendale Sector of—"

"Looking for trouble?"

"We aren't, either of us, Mexicans," Kacey told the two large sentries. "He's as pure as you are."

"As the driven snow," added Jake.

"Wiseass," decided the second sentry.

"He means well," Kacey assured them. "Now, really, I don't

think Colonel Burns, who's a close personal friend of my employer, J. J. Bracken, would want us to be delayed in our mission, fellows."

"Bracken's terrific," said the first sentry.

"Work for him?" asked the second.

"Full time."

"What's he like?"

"A splendid man, exactly as he is on the vidnet."

"Great job, supports the Pure California Coalition cause hundred percent."

"Tells the truth," said the second sentry.

"He'll be pleased to hear what you've had to say." Catching Jake's arm again, she hurried him off along the jungle trail.

After they walked several yards Jake asked her, "Think they'd have shot me if I'd turned out to be Latino?"

"There's really nothing wrong with being proud of one's ethnic heritage, Jake," Kacey told him. "You forget that people who don't have all the privileges and perks that you do need something to give them satisfaction and a sense of purpose. You see—"

"Did you know your great-grandmother's name was Carmelita Sanchez?"

She slowed, frowning up at him. "That's not true."

"Ask your pop sometime."

"You're a very difficult man to interact with," she said. "You have a snide attitude that you adopt whenever you come up against someone you consider, for whatever reason, your inferior."

"True, but I've never shot any of my inferiors with a lazrifle while dressed up in a cute soldier suit."

"You and my father are continually criticizing J. J. Bracken, yet he's a hell of a lot more tolerant than either of you," Kacey said. "Practicing military exercises in a simulated jungle is a perfectly healthy way of—"

"They could join the Boy Scouts and get to march around what real woodlands are still left in SoCal."

They continued on into the simulated jungle. Off among the tall, shadowy trees imitation birds called, and now and then monkeys seemed to chitter.

Eventually Kacey announced, "Here's Path 7. This Hermione Earnshaw, according to what I found out, is lying low in one of the clusters of huts in the Path 7 clearing."

"I'm curious as to why she's lying low."

"Right now, Jake, let's agree that I'm to be in charge of questioning her. You have a real knack for annoying people."

"Yeah, it's taken me years of diligent work to develop that," he said.

AS DAN WAS RETURNING from a twilight run along the beach, Molly's skycar came swooping down to land next to the condo deck.

The young woman, dressed in dark slax and a pullover, jumped from the car and ran to him. "Let's go, c'mon," she urged, catching his hand and tugging.

"Is our destination a surprise," he inquired, allowing her to pull him over to the passenger side, "or are you going to tell me where we're going?"

"I'm pretty sure I know where we'll end up." She gave him a push toward the skycar.

"This is something urgent, huh?"

"I'll explain on the way, Dan. Get in."

Stopping, cupping his hands, he called toward the condo, "Lock up. Tell my dad I'm off gallivanting with Molly."

"Right you are," answered the voice of the home computer while the doors and windows were sliding quietly shut.

Molly, guiding the car up into the growing dusk, told Dan, "This is about my friend Sue Grossman."

Dan poked his tongue into his cheek for a few seconds, eyeing her. "More dangerous visions, is it?"

"No, but she's in trouble, I think. I'm pretty certain of that."

"She phoned you again?"

"It was her father. He asked me if I knew where she was."

"I thought she was the one who never left the house."

"There was some kind of big fight a couple hours ago," answered Molly, concern in her voice. "Not with her father, but with this woman who's living with him. She doesn't care for poor Susan at all."

"You keep getting involved with the affairs of the poor Susans of the world, Molly. Could be you—"

"Quit heckling and let me get on with the explanation of what we're up to, will you?"

"Sorry. But it is true that underdogs and—"

"Possibly that's why I'm so fond of you, poor Daniel," she said. "Sue spent quite a bit of time in a private psychiatric facility run by a nasty fellow named Dr. Stolzer. They got her off Tek, but it was a very rough course of treatment. From what her father said, his lady friend got into a nasty squabble with Sue and ended up threatening to send her back to Stolzer for observation."

"Nasty thing to do."

"Nasty woman, according to Sue. Anyhow, there was some kind of fracas between the two of them and this woman—June Stackpoole is her name, I think—well, she fell down and bumped her head on something and Sue, very upset, went running out of the house. She has a skycar of her own and she jumped in that and took off."

"Couldn't that be good? Go off by herself for a while until everything—"

"There's a tracer in the car," put in Molly. "It was switched off on the outskirts of the Pasadena Sector."

"Proving she doesn't want to be followed."

Molly said, "What I'm afraid of is that she's gone to her favorite Tek parlor, a very exclusive setup in the Pasadena Sector."

"Didn't that occur to her father?"

"No, Mr. Grossman never knew that much about Sue's problems with Tek or any of the other electronic drugs she fooled with," replied Molly. "And when it came time to get her help, he left that to women like this Stackpoole witch."

Turning in his seat, Dan studied her profile. "You intend to bust into this Tek joint and drag her out?"

The day had ended and they were flying through darkness now.

Molly said, "We won't be that flamboyant. This isn't a raid, after all. However, Dan my dear, if Susan is inside that place, I mean to bring her out."

"Has her dad contacted the police?"

"Not yet. My impression is that he'll try to trace her on his own for a while longer and then probably go to a discreet and reliable private investigation service. Less notoriety and publicity that way."

"Not much of a father, sounds to me."

Molly nodded agreement. "We have to find Sue before anybody else does," she told him. "Because if that woman succeeds in putting her away, she won't be able to help us on this case."

"Oh, are we still working on this case?"

"You're damned right we are," Molly said.

14 • THERE

were nine neowood huts in the small clearing in the holographic jungle that the Pure California Coalition used as its main base. Simulated sunlight was shining down on all of them and bright red and yellow flowering bushes climbed over the plank walls and the plaztile roofs. This area was quiet and there seemed to be no one at home in any of the huts.

"That's supposed to be the one she's using." From the edge of the clearing Kacey indicated the cottage with a large 3 hand-lettered on its door.

Stopping her fifty feet or so from the place, Jake slipped out his stungun. "I'll approach with a bit of caution."

"Hermione Earnshaw isn't especially dangerous."

"She may have some dangerous acquaintances." He stood watching the silent hut for a moment.

Touching Kacey's arm and indicating that she stay where she was, Jake moved away into the simulated jungle.

He circled around to the back of the row of huts and moved quietly toward the rear of 3. One good thing about holographic leaves was that they didn't crunch underfoot.

"Damn," he said to himself as he eased nearer.

The back door of the shack wasn't there. It had been ripped off its old-fashioned hinges and tossed into a stretch of simulated brush.

Inching ahead, listening, Jake watched the doorway. The room beyond was thick with shadows.

He sprinted, pressed his back against the neowood wall next to the opening.

Crouched low, stungun in hand, Jake dived over the threshold.

Nothing happened.

Silence surrounded him.

"Damn," he said again. He'd noticed the odor of burned flesh.

He was in the kitchen of the three-room hut. Carefully, Jake made his way to the doorway leading into the living room.

He hesitated, listening, before entering, ducked low.

There was a slender auburn-haired woman sprawled, all askew, on the mattrug. The beams of two lazguns had cut a deep, ugly X across her back, burning away a great swatch of her pale yellow shirt and a good deal of skin and muscle.

He knelt, studying her face.

It was Hermione Earnshaw, no doubt. He'd had pictures of her transmitted from the Cosmos files just an hour ago.

Shaking his head, he went to the front door and reached for the handle.

The door swung in open before he could touch it.

Jake backed, swinging his stungun up.

"Another corpse and here's Cardigan," remarked Lieutenant Drexler.

"What brings you to the jungle, Drexler?" He put his gun away.

"I've been eager to talk to Grossman's assistant," the policeman told him, stepping into the room. "Then I got an unexpected tip that Hermione was holed up down here and in considerable danger. I rushed over, but not in time to prevent you from—"

"C'mon, Lieutenant. She's been dead for at least two hours and you must know, if you queried those toy soldiers at the entrance, that we only arrived here a few minutes ago."

"Perhaps," conceded the cop.

Edging around him, Jake stepped out into the sun-bright clearing.

Kacey, looking uneasy and displeased, was standing, arms folded, about where he'd left her. Two uniformed SoCal Police officers were positioned a few yards from her.

As Jake neared her, Kacey asked him, "What's wrong?"

He leaned close. "Somebody killed her," he answered. "In the back with a lazgun."

"Just like Grossman."

"Pretty similar, yeah."

Kacey stared at the hut. Drexler was in the doorway, summoning the two officers to join him inside. "What did Hermione Earnshaw know that made them kill her?" she said.

"We'll have to find out."

"How?"

Jake shrugged. "That's one of the things I still have to figure out."

.   .   .

THERE WERE a couple hundred people in the main ballroom. Two hundred seventeen, to be exact. Two hundred seventeen people and a good many of them young, handsome, beautiful, and extremely influential. The main ballroom was thick with chatter, laughter, music, and noise, and from its curved viewindows one could see all of Greater Los Angeles far below. This was The Chateau, an airborne private club that circled ten thousand feet above SoCal.

Rowland Burdon, a handsome, dark man of thirty-five, was moving slowly and amiably among the guests. Burdon never drank at his parties, but he frequently popped a pill or a capsule. Always one of the mood drugs his NewTown Pharmaceutical Corporation manufactured. Actually the company was owned by Rowland and his twin sister, Rebecca. And he was, in a leisurely manner that allowed him to chat with the more important guests, heading for the small table where she was sitting, alone and angry.

"Radiating gloom, Sis, is bad for business," Rowland pointed out when he finally reached her and sat opposite.

"Go away, Rollo," she invited, picking up her glass of water.

"The idea, Sis, is this," the brother explained, smiling for the benefit of whoever might be watching. "NewTown specializes in remedies for depression and gloom. Yet you persist in parking here, looking like Death on a bad day, sulking and snarling. All our multitude of friends and business associates are going to say, 'If NewTown's panaceas are so good, how come Becky's in such a sour slump?' We can't—"

"Let me put my request in different terms, Rollo," she cut in. "Take a flying leap for yourself." She sipped at the water. "That could be very impressive from this height."

He put his hand on her wrist and, still smiling, squeezed hard.

"Enough of this shit, Sis," he said in a low voice. "I swear to God that if you don't quit this goddamn sulking, I'll—"

"You'll what, Rollo? Have a couple of thugs shoot me in the back?"

He tightened his grasp, then let go. "What are you hinting at?"

"You killed Dwight Grossman," she said.

"Don't say things like that here. You know I had nothing to do—"

"He's dead. You'll agree to that much, won't you?"

Rowland took a gold-plated pillbox out of his jacket pocket, popped it open, and selected a bright crimson tablet. After swallowing it, he stood up. "We're partners, Sis, equal partners," he reminded her, leaning over the table. "And you know what they say about twins. If something bad happens to one of them, why, the other one feels pain, too. I'd hate to have you suffer."

Rebecca turned away and stared into the blackness outside.

15•BAScom

was back behind his desk. He sat very stiff and still, eyes narrowed, saying nothing.

From her chair Karin Tanoshi said, "It's now nearly twenty minutes past nine P.M."

"Being an excellent detective myself," the chief of the Cosmos Detective Agency told her, "I was already able to figure out what time it was entirely on my own."

"What Karin means," interpreted Roy Anselmo, "is that you called this special meeting for nine, Walt, and that all the rest of the Grossman case team are here—except, as might be expected, Cardigan and Gomez. So why don't we simply—"

"Whilst I was behind stone walls and iron bars, Roy, you were running things," Bascom said. "Now that I am, however fleetingly, on the outside once more, I intend to be in charge."

"I only meant that—"

"We'll wait for them."

Kay Norwood, who was seated close to his desk, leaned toward him and said quietly, "Can you modify the gruffness, Walt?"

"No," he answered, scowling. "Those bastards can't threaten you and not—"

"Has Miss Norwood been threatened?" asked Leo Anson, who was standing near one of the blanked windows.

"We'll get to that," promised Bascom.

The door at the far end of the large office slid open, admitting Gomez and Jake.

"Welcome back, *jefe.*" Gomez worked his way through the scatter of operatives. "Did you get the bouquet I sent you while you were in the lockup? Consisted of roses, violets, pansies, and—"

"Sit down and dummy up," advised his boss.

Moving a chair near the holostage, Jake straddled it. "I'd like to explain, Walt, why we're late."

"No, I want to outline to you all what happened while Kay was ferrying me home from the hoosegow," countered Bascom. "Then I want prelim reports from each of you as to—"

"Before we get to that," interrupted Gomez, who was still on his feet, "you better attend to what we have to say."

"Goddamn it, Sid, don't start talking to me like I'm some rookie operative who just—"

"Whoa, Walt," Jake cut in, "this really is important and has nothing to do with who's in charge here."

"You're telling me you've got something more important than the fact that these bastards will kill Kay if I don't drop this investigation, roll over, and let them railroad me for murder?"

"It's more a question of something that has to be dealt with before we get to that. Trust me on this, will you?"

Kay said, "Walt, I appreciate your concern, but don't push so hard. Listen to Jake and Gomez first."

"All right, okay." Bascom hunched in his chair and nodded at Jake and then his partner. "What is it that has you two lads so riled up?"

Smiling, Gomez perched on the edge of the chief's desk. "Jake and I were comparing notes on our day's activities awhile ago, sir," he began. "It struck us—riled us up, in fact—that we'd been anticipated a good deal. In the interest of our continued survival and well-being, we decided to nose around some."

"You were doing that," said Karin, annoyed, "while we were sitting here and waiting for you to show up."

"*Chiquita,* think of how it hurt me to stay away from you. Nevertheless, stern duty drove me to—"

"Sid," requested Bascom, "less frills."

Jake said, "When I went to talk to the folks at Thelwell, where Grossman worked, I found a hairless lout waiting there to assault me."

"And several of the informants I was planning to call on today," added Gomez, "had been persuaded to set up debilitating booby traps for me."

"Obviously the opposition was aware that the agency would be investigating the Grossman murder," picked up Jake. "But Sid and I concluded that these folks knew our exact itinerary in some instances."

"Although we're not confiding types, *jefe,* we did share some of our plans for today," said Gomez, his left foot swinging slowly back and forth as he spoke. "We reported here on some of what we were intending to—"

"Hold it, you son of a bitch." Anselmo was up out of his chair. "Are you saying, Gomez, that I sold out the—"

"Remain calm," advised Jake. "You're not the one who passed along news to the other side."

"Who is the other side?" asked Bascom.

"We don't know all the players yet," answered Gomez, "but there are definitely Tek *hombres* involved along with—"

"My investigations confirm that," said Anson, moving away from the window. "When we get to our reports, you'll notice—"

"You won't be giving a report, Leo," said Jake.

"What the hell are you talking about, Cardigan?"

"For one thing," said Jake, "we're concerned about how come you deposited $5,000 in that secret account you maintain in the Laguna Sector branch of the Banx system."

"There's nothing secret about that account. And I won the money in a—"

"No, you got it as a fee for collaborating with representatives of some Teklords," corrected Gomez. "Believe me, *cabrón,* I found this all out by consulting two very reliable informants and one world-class stoolpigeon."

"I'm tired of all your wiseass accusations, you greaseball." Anson, head low, came charging at him.

"Violence doesn't solve anything," advised Jake, thrusting out his foot and tripping the husky detective.

Anson stumbled, fell, hit the floor flat out.

Before he could rise, Jake was crouched beside him. He gave him three flat-handed blows to the neck.

Anson yelped, gagged, and dropped into unconsciousness.

Bascom stood up, peering over his desk at the fallen operative. "I assume you lads can prove all this?"

"Oh, *sí*," Gomez assured him. "We even have a couple of very handsome photos."

16 • The

Eternity Depot covered nearly an entire block on the outskirts of the Pasadena Sector. The parking/landing area, thick with sky-cars and landcars tonight, covered an additional acre. The whole complex was intensely and profusely illuminated, the lots and the three-story plastiglass-and-neowood building were beacons in the night.

Susan Grossman had left her skycar nearly a half mile from the immense glowing store. By the time she'd reached the Eternity Depot, she was having some difficulty with her breathing. She'd done virtually no walking lately and she really hadn't been eating all that well. She felt somewhat dizzy. She was frightened, too, as well as ashamed of herself.

She'd promised herself she'd never use Tek again. But after the encounter with Juneanne tonight, she had to do something. She had to make herself feel better.

"Bitch," she said. "Bitch. How can he love that terrible woman?"

There were huge slogans printed across the giant plastiglass front windows of the Eternity Depot in throbbing light tubing: ALL YOUR DEATH NEEDS!, YOU CAN'T BUY A CHEAPER COFFIN ANYWHERE IN GREATER LA!, ON-SITE CREMATION AT LOW, LOW PRICES!, TOMBSTONES ALWAYS AT LEAST 20% OFF!

A robot doorman, painted dead white, wearing a long black robe with a cowl and holding a scythe, greeted Susan as she, breathing shallowly, approached an entrance. "Welcome to the Eternity Depot, young miss," he said. "You look downcast and depressed. In mourning, are you?"

"Yes," she replied, "for myself."

"Suicidal, perhaps? You might want to look around our Suicide Club annex."

Susan quietly told him, "No, I want to see the second assistant manager."

"Ah, that's one way to cheer up." The black-clad bot winked at her, eyelid clicking metallically. "You'll find him in Room 5 on Level 2 this evening."

Thanking the grim robot, the young woman entered the brightly lit coffin showroom that lay beyond the entryway.

Mournful organ music was being piped in through a scatter of ebony speakers floating up near the deep gray ceiling.

"Something for yourself?" inquired the handsome blond android salesman who came gliding over to her. "Or perhaps for a loved one?"

"I can think of a couple of loved ones I'd like to see in coffins," she admitted. "But tonight I want the second level."

The dark-suited andy politely pointed. "You'll find the ramp just to the left of the display of Wormproof Low-Budget Burial Boxes, miss."

The door to Room 5 was black. It was partially concealed by a stack of neowood crates full of urns.

Susan knocked twice, paused, knocked once.

The door, with a faint creaking, slid aside.

The small room she entered smelled strongly of dead flowers and some kind of pungent incense.

She sneezed.

"Little Susie," said a voxbox in the ceiling. "Long time no see, sweetie."

"I've been away."

"Welcome back. The usual?"

She nodded. "There's maybe a slight problem. I—"

"Can't pay?"

"Not tonight, but I'll be able to—"

"No problem, Susie. You've been a good customer and we know you're good for it."

"Thanks."

"Don't mention it. Use Crib 11. That's on the left."

"I remember."

A door in the far wall creaked open.

She didn't immediately move.

"Go ahead, sweetie," urged the voxbox.

"I was going to quit this stuff. I was."

"Hell, that turned out to be a stupid decision, didn't it?"

"Yes," she said finally. She crossed and stepped through the doorway.

Crib 11 was warm and cozy, with a small fire crackling in the simulated fireplace. The walls seemed to be made of neatly fitted logs, and out the window was a simulated view of a tranquil woodland scene in the late afternoon.

Susan, fists clenched, remained a long time just inside the room.

The cot was wide, covered with a bright plaid plyoblanket. Next to it was a low table on which rested the familiar Tek gear. The compact Brainbox, the headset, and—five, she counted—five Tek chips.

"I stopped," she reminded herself. "I stopped and I thought it was all over."

But she'd been hurting so much lately.

She had to do something to stop that.

Crossing, she sat down on the cot.

In the woods outside a single bird began to sing.

Susan, hand shaking a little, picked up the headset and adjusted it to her skull.

She poked at the cockroach-sized Tek chips, sorting them. Selecting one, she inserted it in the Brainbox.

She activated the box and stretched out on the cot, closing her eyes. "I wasn't going to do this anymore," she said.

GOMEZ LEANED an elbow on the railing of Jake's deck and studied the misty night and the black ocean. "Ah, to be young once again," he observed with a sigh.

From his deck chair, Jake said, "You're referring to my son?"

"Sure, Dan's out on the town with the lovely Molly while you and I vegetate here and talk shop."

"On a school night, too."

"My own youth," said Gomez, "seems to be receding at an increasingly alarming rate, *amigo.*"

"Hard work is the cure for that sort of thing."

"Okay, *sí,* we'll get back to the case." His partner turned his back on the Pacific Ocean. "I, with the *jefe*'s blessing, will be embarking for Texas *mañana* early in search of the gifted and elusive Avram Moyech."

Jake stretched up out of the chair. "Appears I'll be remaining in Greater LA and digging further into the life and times of Dwight Grossman."

Gomez knuckled his misty mustache. "There has to be more to this *guisado* than just Tek shenanigans," he said. "I know, *sí*, that once we persuaded the double-crossing Anson to confide in us, he explained that he'd been on the payroll of some Tek cartel underlings from the NorCal area. But my feeling is that Grossman was sent on to glory for more complex sins than annoying a Teklord."

"Bascom's going to cover the NorCal angle himself. We can—"

"You think turning our fallen colleague over to the estimable Lieutenant Drexler will take some of the heat off the chief?"

"Need more than the confession of a bit player like Anson to convince Drexler that Bascom's not a crazed killer," said Jake. "He doesn't think much of us, either."

"You're wrong there, *amigo*," corrected Gomez. "Now and then I've noticed the lieutenant gazing at me with that kind of look young boys reserve for sports heroes."

Jake grinned. "Maybe you're right, Sid. You well could be the guy's role model, his idol."

"Looks and brains. That's what impresses the multitude."

"Phone call," announced the voice of the condo computer.

"Take a message," suggested Jake, not moving.

"I advise you to respond to this one, sir."

Jake said, "Hold on, Sid." He went into the living room.

The vidphone screen was blank. A thin, nervous male voice asked, "You're on a tap-proof phone, aren't you, Cardigan?"

"Yeah. Who are you?"

"This is about Hermione Earnshaw."

Jake sat in the chair facing the screen. "Okay, let's hear it."

"You have to come and see me."

"Not unless I know a hell of a lot more about you and the setup."

Silence followed. Nearly a full minute of it.

Then the phonescreen made a faint humming noise. The image of a slender black man of about forty snapped into view. He was sitting on the edge of a silver chair in front of a blank gray wall. "My name is Sam Hopkins," he began. "You're certain your phone is tap-proof?"

"It is. And my condo isn't bugged. What do you know about her death?"

Hopkins hesitated. "I know why she was killed," he said finally.

"Suppose you tell me now?"

"You've got to come out here. I don't want to stay on the phone that long," he said, glancing offscreen. "I'm staying at a friend's place here in the NewTown Sector and—"

"Whoa now, that's a rough area," cut in Jake, shaking his head. "A completely private township with its own cops and—"

"I know what Hermione and Grossman knew."

"How'd you come by that?"

"I'm the one who provided the information that got them both killed."

"Give me your address," said Jake.

SUSAN'S FATHER WAS a trim, handsome man of forty-five. He smiled, slipped an arm around her shoulders as they walked away from the tennis court at the rear of their mansion.

"I thought I'd win that one," he said, hugging her. "Congratulations."

"It was close, Dad," she said, laughing.

They strolled up to the terrace and sat at one of the small tables. "What would you like to drink, princess?"

She felt, briefly, tearful. "You haven't called me that in a long while."

"I regret that, Sue," her father told her. "While that terrible woman was here, I simply ceased to think clearly."

"She's gone, gone for good and all," reminded his daughter. "Pretty soon we'll forget that Juneanne was ever here."

"That's what I'm hoping."

"Shall I call a butler to—"

"Who's that down by the courts?" He half rose from his chair, eyes narrowing.

Susan turned to look, then inhaled sharply. "It's them. It's them."

A slight red-haired man and a large hairless man were walking up across the simulated green lawn. They were laughing and now, realizing they'd been spotted, they both waved.

"Are these fellows friends of yours, princess?"

"No, they're not. They . . . they're the ones who killed Dwight."

He frowned at her. "So you do know something about that?" he said. "Juneanne told me you were involved, but I didn't want to believe that. Now it turns out that—"

"It was them, Dad. I tried to stop it but—"

"How could you have stopped them from killing your brother? Were you there when—"

"No, but I saw it."

"Good God, Sue, are you going to start that psychic nonsense again?"

She made fists of her hands, saying, "This isn't going right. This isn't the Tek dream I—"

"Hiya, Susie," said the redhead as he hopped up onto the terrace stones. "We're here to take care of your problems."

"No, I don't want you to do a damn thing. Go away."

The hairless man's laugh was high pitched. "You want us to kill Juneanne *and* your father, kid."

"And you ordered two of the deluxe coffins for them," added his partner.

"Stop it," she cried. "I don't want this."

The hairless man said, "You've got no idea of everything you're going to get, kid."

Reaching out, he yanked the headset off her head.

She sat up on the cot and cried out.

He was still there. He smiled and took hold of both her arms.

17 • THERE

was nothing in the parlor except two metal chairs.

Sam Hopkins sat in one, Jake straddled the other.

The one-way viewindow showed a matching row of identical small, square houses outside in the foggy night. The artificial bay was downhill with thick mist drifting in across its dark waters.

"The friend who's letting me use this place just moved in," the black man was explaining. "Hence the lack of furnishings."

Jake said, "I don't like the NewTown Sector. I don't want to hang around any longer than I have to."

Hopkins glanced toward the window. "I hate NewTown myself," he acknowledged, "but if you work for NewTown Pharmaceuticals, you pretty much have to reside here."

"That's who you work for, huh?"

"Yes, in Promotion & Publicity." He laughed a thin, dry laugh. "Ironic, considering what I've been up to lately."

"How'd you know to contact me, Hopkins?"

"Hermione Earnshaw mentioned your name. She was planning to contact you, I believe, but then . . ." He rubbed his thin fingers over the bridge of his nose a few times.

"She was a friend of yours?"

"We actually lived together for nearly six months—year before last. I should have stayed with her." He glanced at the window again. "Let me start off by explaining, Cardigan, that I don't know as much about the situation as Grossman did. But because of what I told Hermione . . . well, both of them are dead."

"So what exactly did you tell her?"

Hopkins asked, "Do you know anything about something called SinTek?"

"Not a damn thing."

"The Burdons—that's Rowland and Rebecca Burdon, the twin tycoons who run NewTown Pharmaceuticals—the Burdons arranged nearly a year ago with both state and federal authorities to try to develop a safe electronic drug. A synthetic one that will deliver the gratifying fantasies that real Tek provides its users. But, and this was the selling point, the damn stuff isn't addictive. Not even habit-forming. Plus which, it doesn't have any of the terrible side effects that Tek does—no brain damage from prolonged addiction, no seizures or blackouts."

"Sounds like another miracle of science and technology," commented Jake. "How far along are they?"

After checking the window again, Hopkins answered, "Lord knows if they'll ever have a product to sell. The point is that SinTek is only a cover-up. NewTown has built a special Design &

Research facility out of state, but it's devoted to more than per-
fecting a safe synthetic substitute for Tek."

Jake hunched his shoulders, frowning. "C'mon, you're saying
they're manufacturing the real stuff on the side?"

"That's it, exactly," said Hopkins. "Anyone inspecting the
setup sees SinTek only, but in the underground sections of the
place they're turning out street-quality Tek."

"The Tek cartels don't take kindly to amateurs going into competition with them."

Hopkins told him, "I'm fairly certain Rowland Burdon got one
of the big NorCal Tek cartels to go into partnership on this whole
damn project."

"Which one?"

"That I haven't learned."

"But Dwight Grossman found out, huh?"

"That's what Hermione told me," he said. "I knew she and
Grossman were preparing a series of reports on the big SoCal drug
companies. I told Hermione what I knew and what I suspected.
After she passed that along to him, Grossman obviously did considerable investigating on his own."

"Was he planning to put all he learned into his report for
Thelwell?"

Shaking his head, Hopkins said, "I suspect that Grossman,
who wasn't an especially nice guy—"

"So I've heard."

"I think he was contemplating trying to collect a substantial fee
to keep quiet."

"That wasn't too bright of him."

Hopkins lowered his voice. "Listen, I don't think anyone's on
to me yet at NewTown Pharmaceuticals," he said. "But if things
start to go bad, can you—Christ!"

The door of the parlor suddenly came flying into the room.

Three men, all in the uniform of the NewTown Private Police Force, charged in in the wake of the fallen door.

"This is an illegal meeting, convened to conspire to commit criminal acts," announced the highest-ranking intruder, a lean sergeant. "You both are being arrested, under the NewTown penal code section that—"

"Hold it, folks." Jake was on his feet. "Do you make-believe cops have a warrant for breaking into this—"

"Looks like this guy is resisting arrest," said the lean sergeant to one of the other officers.

"Without a doubt, sir." He swung the stungun in his hand three inches to the left and shot Jake.

THE AMPLE BLOND ANDROID in the black bathing suit said, "It's never too early to think about dying."

"Very true," agreed Dan.

He and Molly were in one of the coffin showrooms of the Eternity Depot.

"Now, these three models here, including the one that plays favorite hymns around the clock," continued the android salesperson, "you can buy on easy installments that even school kids such as yourselves can afford."

"Actually, in point of fact," said Molly, "we came here to see the Second Assistant Manager."

"Really?" The blonde scratched her backside and looked disappointed. "Nice clean-cut kids such as yourselves, and you want to indulge in . . . Well, that's none of my darned business, now, is it? No, not at all. 'Pamela, you just work here, kid. Keep in mind that you're nothing more than an android, a collection of nuts and bolts without a soul or—' "

"How do we find him?" asked Molly impatiently.

"Level 2, Door 5." She rubbed her believable hands together dismissively and turned away from them.

As they headed up to the next level of the vast store, Dan said, "Did you see any of the coffins that you really liked?"

"Saw one I might pop you into if you don't cease trying to be the Gomez of your generation."

"Sid's a very clever guy and—"

"For them as cherishes clever guys. Me, I like your type better."

When they located Door 5, Molly said, "I hope the ritual Susan told me about a while ago still prevails."

She tapped the door twice, waited, then tapped once more.

Creaking and scraping, the door moved open.

"Newcomers," said the overhead voxbox. "Lovebirds, no doubt."

Molly took hold of Dan's hand and smiled up at the speaker in the ceiling. "We'd like to share a crib, sir."

"That'll be $300, kiddies."

Dan said, "$300 just to—"

"That'll be fine. I have the Banx chits right here." Molly reached into her pocket and produced a handful of money.

"Just toss 'em on the floor and head through the door yonder. You're in Crib 14. Enjoy."

"Thank you, sir."

A door in the opposite wall rattled open.

Hand in hand, Molly and Dan entered the corridor. As the door grated shut behind them, a young woman screamed behind one of the crib doors.

"That's Susan," said Molly, starting to run.

18 • THERE

was a pain all across his upper chest—a sharp, needling pain.

Jake made a groaning noise, rubbing his palm across his chest. The pain kept on.

Very slowly, as he became aware of other pains in other parts of his body, Jake started moving toward full consciousness.

He was, he now realized, sprawled flat on his back on something fairly soft.

He opened his eyes very gingerly and was assaulted by pinkish light and images of rose petals and twining leaves and vines.

Wincing, he shut his eyes again for protection.

New pain started gripping at his stomach and he felt dizzy.

"Stungun," he recalled. And he was experiencing the usual aftereffects.

Carefully, cautiously, Jake risked opening his eyes a second time.

The walls were indeed decorated with a pattern of flowering rosebushes.

There was also a delicate rosebud scent lingering in the air.

Aloud, in a dry, rusty voice, Jake speculated, "What the hell sort of jail is this?"

After keeping his eyes open for a couple of minutes, Jake decided he might attempt to sit up.

He'd awakened on a wide oval bed, one that was covered with a soft, pale pink thermoquilt.

He noticed now that, although fully clothed, his boots were missing.

Concentrating, working to keep all the assorted pains from overwhelming him, Jake succeeded in sitting up.

Next, groaning and muttering, he swung his bare feet over the side of the bed.

For a while he felt very wobbly and the roses started chasing each other around the walls.

Gradually, though, Jake regained control of himself.

This was definitely a bedroom he'd awakened into. In his limited experience with the police of the NewTown Sector he'd never actually been in one of their jail cells. But he didn't think any of them were furnished like this.

Confidence returning, he placed both feet on the thick red carpeting and stood.

His left leg refused to function. Jake went falling to the floor with a thud.

"Why the heck didn't you call me if you wanted to try this?"

Coming through the doorway, wearing a rose-colored slaxsuit, was Kacey Bascom. She hurried to him, offered her hand.

"Begone, shoo," he suggested, waving off any assistance from her.

"What, then—are you planning to sit there on your stubborn backside for the rest of the night?"

"Eventually I intend to rise," Jake informed her. "Entirely unaided. Why, by the way, am I in your damned bedroom, Kacey?"

"Lot better than a cell, wouldn't you say?"

"Remains to be seen. Are you affiliated with the NewTown cops?"

"That's a nasty thing to accuse anybody of." She stood, studying him. "If you'd take my hand, I'll get you upright again and put you in a chair in my living room so we—"

"Explain first where I am and exactly why."

"Obviously this is my house in the Westwood Sector."

"And why didn't I wake up in the clutches of the NewTown vigilance committee?"

"It took a lot of arranging, but I finally got the NewTown Sector board of supervisors to—"

"Backtrack." By using the bed and ignoring his collection of pains, Jake was able to pull himself to a standing position eventually. "Go ahead, explain."

"Oh, sorry. I got fascinated watching you display your intense stubbornness," Kacey said, smiling faintly. "Once you were arrested, I set about to finagle you out of jail. That's all, simple."

"Where's that chair you were touting?"

She reached for him. "Next room. Here, I'll help you to—"

"Just indicate the location. I feel in the mood to sit a spell."

Shrugging in resignation, she returned to the living room

and left him to follow her. "You have a choice of seating arrangements."

He settled for the nearest one, a plump yellow armchair. "Where are my boots, Kacey?"

"Right behind you, next to the bedroom door."

Jake managed, without falling seriously out of the yellow chair, to retrieve the boots and start tugging them back on. "Explain how you knew I was in the NewTown jug."

"Well, I'd followed you from your condo to the NewTown Sector, and when the local cops—"

"Nope, no," he interrupted. "Nobody followed me. Nary a soul."

Kacey perched on the arm of the white sofa. "Okay, I was tipped off. Because of my political connections, I have people in the NewTown establishment who—"

"What's my current status? Am I out on bail or—"

"You are as free as a bird, that's your status. Thanks to me, all charges were dropped."

He watched her for a moment. "You didn't have anything to do with that raid, did you?"

"I told you I'm not affiliated with the NewTown cops. They're a shade too conservative even for me," Kacey assured him.

"Would the Burdons be among the folks you know in the New-Town Sector?"

"I know who they are, but we're not friends. I do have a few friends who're executives with NewTown Pharmaceuticals, though."

Nodding, Jake asked her, "What about Hopkins?"

"Who?"

"Sam Hopkins. He was in that apartment with me when the cops busted in."

Kacey's brow furrowed. "The police report claims you were arrested for operating a skycar while under the influence of stimulants."

Jake said, "Damn, what did they do with the guy?"

"Maybe I can find out. See, I never heard of him until just now," she said. "Tell me something about him."

"Hopkins works for NewTown Pharmaceuticals in the Publicity wing," said Jake. "Forty or thereabouts, on the slim side. He's black and—"

"Then they might've taken him to the Colored Holding Facility."

"I haven't heard of that."

"The Pure California Coalition is very strong in NewTown and they got that through last year. Actually, it's a very comfortable sort of—"

"Yeah, I'm sure. Can you find out about him? If Hopkins is still above the sod, I want to have another talk with him."

"Why do you suspect he's not alive?"

"Dwight Grossman's defunct, so is Hermione Earnshaw," Jake explained. "Hopkins is the lad who prompted them to investigate certain activities. That got them killed."

Leaving the sofa, she crossed to stand over him. "This all ties in with my father, then—with why he was framed?"

"All a part of the same package, yeah," he said. "Where did my skycar end up?"

"It was towed here. You'll find it out in the landing area."

Standing up in a wobbly, swaying way, Jake told her, "I think I'll head for home, Kacey."

"Not yet." She pushed him, gently, and he sat again. "You're still too shaky for solo flying. More important, you're going to have to tell me everything you learned from this Hopkins guy."

"If you know much more, Kacey, they'll put you on the shit list, too."

"Don't be a ninny, I've probably been on it from the start. Walt Bascom is my father, remember?" she said. "Besides, we made a deal to work together, which means sharing information."

"Okay," agreed Jake. "Sit yourself, don't interrupt, and I'll fill you in."

19 • SPRINTing

ahead of Molly, Dan reached the door to Crib 11 before her.

He took hold of the handle, turning it. When the door started to open, Dan booted it.

As the door went flapping inward, Dan, yanking out his academy stungun, hunched down.

Inside the cozy crib, Susan Grossman cried out again in pain.

Ducked low, Dan lunged into the room.

The large hairless man, giving a high-pitched grunt, lifted Susan high and hurled her into the oncoming young man.

She hit him hard, shoulder digging into his chest, right hand slapping across his face, just as he was about to aim his stungun.

Both she and Dan went falling back through the doorway and into the shadowy corridor.

Now from his shoulder holster the hairless man ripped out his lazgun. Snarling, he took three steps forward. "You little bastards are going to cease to be," he promised in his piping voice.

His right arm stretched out rigid, the barrel of the gun pointed right at the tangled Dan.

But then Molly jumped into view, her stungun held in both hands. "Not just yet," she informed him as she fired.

His empty eyebrows climbed, his eyes went rolling backward into his head. The gun hand snapped up and, his trigger finger spasmodically flexing and unflexing, the lazgun fired twice. Its sizzling beam ate two smoking jagged holes in the low crib ceiling.

An alarm started hooting in the corridor.

Staggering backward, arms flapping, the hairless man sat on the bed, tottered, rocked back and forth, then dropped over onto the floor, out cold.

Molly dashed into the crib, bent over the sprawled man, and did a quick frisk. "No ID at all," she said disappointedly, moving up and away.

Dan, on his feet, was helping Susan to stand.

She said, "We've got to get out of here. That alarm'll bring all sorts of nasty folks onto the scene." She pointed at the far end of the passway. "There's a back way out of here. Let's, please, hurry."

"We'll retreat," agreed Dan, catching hold of Molly's hand.

The three of them went running.

HIS SKYCAR SET on an automatic homeward course, Jake was leaning back in the pilot seat. The aftereffects of having been stungunned were, not quite as rapidly as he might have wished, leaving him. By morning he ought to feel fit again.

"As fit as a weather-beaten codger has any right to feel," he said.

The phonescreen spoke to him. "Call from your son."

"Let's have it."

Dan, looking excited, appeared on the small rectangular screen in the dash. "Can you get over here right away, Dad?"

After taking in the details of the room Dan was phoning from, Jake said, "Looks like you're at Molly's."

"I am," confirmed his son. "I haven't had a chance to talk to you since this morning, but we've come across something damned important. It has to do with the case you're working on, with the murder Bascom's accused of."

"Listen, Dan—at least one Tek cartel is tied in with this," he told him. "You and Molly have to be damned cautious about poking into—"

"Can we, maybe, Dad, have the paternal lecture *after* I tell you what we know. We may be working against a deadline here."

Grinning, making a go-ahead gesture toward the screen, Jake invited, "Proceed."

"Some of this stuff is going to sound very strange to you. It did to me," began Dan. "I'll fill in that background when you get here to the Beverly Hills Sector. The important thing is that Molly's a pretty good friend of Susan Grossman and—"

"You're talking about Dwight Grossman's sister?"

"That Susan Grossman, yes," said Dan, impatient. "She's here at Molly's with us. She saw the killing and can identify the two men who killed her brother. Fact, we already got a make on one of them, but he's dead. The other one, a big guy with no hair to speak of, we ran into tonight when we pulled Susan out of a Tek parlor."

"The hairless lout I've met myself," said Jake, nodding. He punched out an alternate course on the control panel. "Was Susan Grossman there when they shot her brother?"

"Not exactly. That's one of the odd things about this," said Dan. "Are you coming over?"

"You've aroused my curiosity," Jake told him. "See you in about ten minutes."

THE HOUSE WAS nearly two hundred years old and had been built to resemble a Spanish villa. The large living room had a beamed ceiling of real wood and the floor was of real tile.

Jake was pacing across the yellow and blue tiles, passing close to the arched windows that looked out on an immense illuminated swimming pool that was ringed by several dozen real palm trees. "I suppose," he said slowly, "it's possible."

"You saw the pictures Rex got for us," said Dan. "They match her descriptions."

"That they do," admitted Jake. "And the lout with the absence of hair looks pretty much like the guy I tangled with at Thelwell." He returned to the low oaken coffee table on which had been spread the pictures Molly and Dan had acquired from Rex/ GK-30. "I've heard of the redhead before. Leroy Salten. Yeah, a freelance gunman who'd work for just about anybody."

Susan was sitting alone, very still, on the sofa. "I don't know why I developed this . . . knack," she said softly. "Some people call this sort of ability a gift. I don't, though, look at it that way."

Picking up one photo of each man, Jake moved closer to her. "You never saw either of these guys before?"

"Never, no, Mr. Cardigan. Not until I had the vision of their killing my brother last night."

"We sure all saw the bald guy tonight," put in Molly as she

went over to sit beside her forlorn friend. "He was trying to kill Sue."

Susan shook her head. "I'm not really certain of that," she said in her faraway voice. "From the little he said before you two came to help me, I think he was planning to take me somewhere."

"He didn't say where?" asked Jake.

"No, I'm sorry."

Dan said, "How did they know Susan was going to be at the Eternity Depot tonight?"

"We've got Teklords mixed up in this whole business." Jake resumed pacing, slapping the photos, absently, against his leg. "Once she showed up at that Tek emporium, somebody passed the information along."

"But why," asked Molly, "do they want to hurt her?"

"Could be they've heard she claims to have information on the killing," said Jake. "Or they may just figure she knows what he knew."

Susan asked him, "Was my brother involved with Tek in some way? Was it because of my . . . of my being hooked on the stuff for so long?"

"He was doing research for some reports on the pharmaceutical outfits in Greater LA," answered Jake, halting beside one of the big windows. "There's a link there somewhere with the Tek trade. He didn't mention any of that to you, Susan?"

Her smile was small and fleeting. "I haven't seen much of Dwight for a long while, Mr. Cardigan," she replied. "After my stay with . . . with Dr. Stolzer in his rehab facility . . . well, that made my brother very uneasy. He didn't feel having a Tekhead for a sister was going to help him in his career. He never visited me while I was there and . . . once I came home, my father thought it best if I didn't see too many people for a while. Not that Dwight was fighting to visit me."

"Does your father know anything about what Dwight was working on?"

"I don't believe they've been in touch for weeks," she said. "My brother wasn't especially fond of Juneanne Stackpoole. She's my father's . . . um . . . female companion. He made the mistake of telling Dad what he thought of her and . . . since my father is probably the only man in Greater Los Angeles who doesn't realize what a terrible woman she is . . . well, it led to an argument and somewhat of a falling-out."

Dan said, "Let's get back to what Susan experienced, her vision of the killing. Obviously that's not evidence, but I'm convinced it was accurate. She really did, I don't know how, have some kind of psychic glimpse of what went on last night."

"That won't mean a damn thing to the police," said Jake. "In fact, even after what you've told me, I'm still a mite skeptical myself."

"What do you think we're doing?" asked his son. "Running a con on you?"

"I'm saying it's hard to accept something this unusual." He moved closer to Susan. "How long have you been able to do this?"

"It's not something I can do," answered the young woman. "It's more like something that's done to me. These scenes, these glimpses of what's going on someplace else—they simply hit me all of a sudden. Like, you know, a seizure or a fit."

"You can't control one, summon up an image?"

"No, and I can't tune in on something as if it were a vidnet show." Sighing out a breath, she leaned back on the sofa. "I've thought about this a lot—and done quite a bit of reading, too—since I started having these visions. They got going right after I came home from Dr. Stolzer's facility. Either all that Tek I used quirked my brain in a strange way or Dr. Stolzer's electronic treatments caused a change in some of my brain cells. Supposedly brain injuries have been known to let psychic abilities loose. I also considered the possibility I was simply crazy, but the fact that what I see turns out to be true convinced me I'm not."

Jake said, "Back when I was using Tek—five, six years ago—I ran into three or four people who claimed they'd developed psionic powers from using the stuff. I never saw any proof of it, though."

"Nobody believes a Tekhead. That's why I haven't told anybody—except Molly. And then Dan and you, Mr. Cardigan," she said, looking up at him. "When you said you used to be hooked on Tek, was that just to make me feel I'm not the only idiot in—"

"No, I had a serious problem with Tek," he told her. "But I don't anymore."

"How'd you quit?"

"It was very rough. I did it mostly on my own, without any medical or psych help," he said. "But Dan helped me and so did my partner Sid Gomez. Neither of them let me kid myself about what I was really doing."

Susan said, "I don't know if I can stop. I thought I could. Then tonight I got so upset—and, damn it, there I was, back at that place."

"You'll get to a point where no matter how bad reality gets, you won't turn to Tek."

"I don't have the kind of people in my life that you apparently did, Mr. Cardigan."

"First off, you've got yourself," he said. "You've also got Molly and Dan—and you've got me."

20 • JAKE

kissed the pretty blond woman, then stepped back. "Actually, Bev," he said, "I'm also here on business."

Bev Kendricks smiled, moved around behind her desk, and sat down. "That was a sort of businesslike kiss, now that I think about it."

"No, that was the romantic portion of this get-together." He straddled a chair. "Now comes the business."

The offices of Bev's private detective agency were in a towering commercial building that was built out over the Pacific in the Santa Monica Sector. From her high, wide windows one could see the ocean and the early-morning fog, still floating above the pale blue water.

"I heard Walt Bascom is out of jail," she said. "Even though we're rivals, I admire him. With some reservations."

"He's out for now, yeah," said Jake. "We still have to find out who killed Dwight Grossman."

"How can I help?"

"The Burdon twins figure in this mess somehow," he told her. "As I recall, you know them."

"Mostly I'm casual friends with Rebecca, better known as the lesser of two Burdons," answered the private investigator. "She's far less nasty than Rowland. As a matter of fact, Rebecca loaned me part of the money when I decided to start up my own agency."

"Okay, she's a pal, but what about the operations of NewTown Pharmaceuticals? Anything shady there that you know about?"

Frowning, Bev answered, "I don't believe the Burdons are crooks, if that's what you're asking. And certainly not murderers."

He hunched his shoulders slightly. "NewTown is working on a supposedly harmless version of Tek. The working title is SinTek," he said. "Heard anything about it?"

"Nothing, no. But then I haven't talked to Rebecca that much over the past few months," she answered. "You think Grossman's death has something to do with this imitation Tek?"

"Too soon to tell."

Turning, she looked briefly out into the brightening morning. "What do you suspect, Jake, that the Burdons are actually manufacturing the real thing? That SinTek is just a cover for an illegal operation?"

"It's a possibility that's been suggested to me," he replied. "By seemingly reliable sources."

She faced him again, shaking her head. "Not Rebecca, she wouldn't go along with anything like that. That company was founded by her grandfather and she—"

"How about her brother?"

"Well, Rowland is a very aggressive guy. But, no, I don't see him sidelining in Tek."

Jake asked, "Why haven't you been in touch with Rebecca Burdon very much of late?"

"She's been spending a lot of time in the Caribbean, and whatever she's doing down there, it apparently doesn't leave her much time to phone or be phoned," said Bev. "Honestly now, Jake, she isn't the sort of person to—"

"Why the Caribbean?"

"She likes it there, I suppose."

"I have some digging to do at Cosmos." Jake stood up. "Soon as this case is over, we'll—"

"After this case, there'll be another one," she said. "But do look me up the next time you're in a romantic mood, no matter how fleeting, Jake."

"You're very near the top of my list," he assured her as he left the office.

THE COMPUTER SAID, "No, really, Jake, you can level with me. Give me, I'd appreciate it, your honest opinion."

Jake was sitting in one of the pale green plastiglass research cubicles in the Cosmos Detective Agency's InfoCenter. There were six large compscreens mounted on the wall in front of his seat. "It's okay, Alec," he said after taking another small sip from the plyomug on his work desk.

"I was expecting a more enthusiastic response to my homemade cappuccino nearcaf."

"Alec, you're a computer and this is an office situation. So the word *homemade* doesn't actually apply." He tapped the control panel. "Okay. Now let us return to fishing for information on the NewTown Pharmaceuticals folks. Specifically, I want stuff about any new plants and facilities built within the past two years or so."

"If our homemade nearcaf operation doesn't catch on, you lugs will have to send out again."

"The cappuccino is great. Hits the spot. C'mon, and provide me with—"

"Having a nozzle installed can be painful, you know," continued the computer. "But, feeling that no sacrifice is too great for you lads, I—"

"NewTown," repeated Jake.

"Okay, ignore my efforts at hospitality. Take a gander at Screen 5. That's the facade of the NewTown Research & Design Complex put up last summer in Lisbon, Portugal. Trite design, rather obviously reminiscent of the work of the late-twenty-first-century architectural whiz, Piet Goedewaagen. Though cheapened by the holographic—"

"What else do we have, Alec?"

"Screen 4 gives you a glimpse of the Project Development Facility on the island of San Peligro. Erected a year and a half ago. Note the artificial palm trees swaying in the balmy Caribbean breeze."

Jake grinned. "Get me floor plans and area background on this one," he requested. "Employee roster and any data about materials and equipment shipped there."

"Sounds like this is a bingo."

"A near bingo at least."

Jake, after trying his tepid nearcaf again, said, "I'd also like you to check through all the NewTown employees in all their operations worldwide. Can you do that?"

"Certainly, but since it's not entirely legal or kosher, it'll take a minute longer," answered the computer. "You looking for somebody in particular?"

Placing the simulated photo of the hairless assassin facedown on the computer's scanpad, Jake suggested, "Like to know if this goon is on any of their payrolls—or ever was."

"Not a very prepossessing chap."

The computer made a dry clacking sound for nearly fifteen seconds. "Look at Screen 3."

The image of a large, thickset man with curly brown hair and a fuzzy mustache was showing there.

Jake narrowed his eyes, studying the photo. "Yeah, that could very well be him under that wig."

"Here. This is how he looks without it and the lip fuzz."

A revised portrait appeared, this time of a hairless man.

Jake nodded. "That's him. Who is he?"

"Summerson, Malcolm, age thirty-seven, unmarried. No criminal record. He's been with NewTown a little over three years and works out of the Frisco office in a security capacity. Former Oregon State Militia officer."

"Where can I find him?"

"Summerson resides in San Mateo in NorCal at . . . No, whoops. He moved out of there early this very morning. No forwarding address."

"Print me out everything you've got on this lout."

"No problem, Jake. And how about a fresh cup of—hold on. Message for you on Screen 2."

Bascom, sitting cross-legged atop his cluttered desk, materialized on the compscreen. "There's been another death, Jake," he said. "The Long Beach Sector cops found Sam Hopkins dead on the sand a little after six this morning."

"Shit," observed Jake. "How was he killed?"

"They're saying suicide . . ."

"Yeah, he was probably remorseful about getting stungunned and dragged out of his place by the NewTown lawmen."

"Eventually, Jake, I'll have a copy of the *true* autopsy," promised the agency head. "Then we'll know what really did him in and whether they used anything to make him talk before bumping him off."

"If Hopkins was persuaded to talk, then the opposition is aware we know about SinTek and what it's a cover-up for." Jake leaned ahead in his chair. "I'm planning to embark for the colorful Caribbean later today. And you?"

"Up to Frisco to trace the Tek connection," answered Bascom. "Strive to remain alive."

21 • The

naked young woman seated herself before the dressing-room mirror. After considering the five wigs scattered on the small plastiglass table, she selected a bright red one and began fitting it over her close-cropped blond hair. "Darn sakes, Marney," she said, addressing her image, "what's somebody with your batch of talents doin' in a dump like this—in the Texas Territory, for cryin' out loud? Once upon a time out west you were a—*hey!*"

The neowood door had come flapping open. "Do I have the pleasure of addressing Pistol Packin' Marney?" inquired the large, wide black man who pushed in, smiling.

"Heck almighty!" Marney jumped up, grabbing the kimono off

the back of her chair and starting to slip into it. "Haven't you ever heard of somethin' called privacy?"

"Every hour on the hour you go out there and, after singing, dancing, and giving an exhibition of trick shooting, you do a strip," the intruder reminded her. His right arm was made of silvery metal and he began massaging it now, as though it were giving him pain. "So being observed in a state of undress ought not to faze you."

"Darn sakes, that's show business out in the club, an' this here is my private dressin' room, an' what in the holy heck is the idea of your bargin' in like a—"

"I'm your new agent, Marney," he explained, shutting the door behind him and approaching her.

"I already got one rude an' crude agent, which is more than plenty."

"Oh, but you need me, Marney." He held out his metallic right hand.

Very reluctantly, she shook it. "I would like it very much if you'd just up an' get the—*yow!*" An electric shock had gone jumping from his hand to hers. She pulled free of his silvery grip, turned her back on him, and sat again in the chair. "What in the almighty heck was that for?"

"A sample of what you might experience," he answered. "Keep in mind, Marney, that what you got was the lowest setting."

"What the darn heck do you want?"

"My name is Sam Cimarron," he said. "When I'm not acting as a talent agent, I serve in assorted capacities for Sleeper Farris."

"Oh, heck," she said. "I only owe Sleeper somethin' tiny. The amount still due on my loan isn't more than—"

"$15,900."

"It can't, nope, be anythin' like that."

"Well, you haven't been keeping up your weekly payments for a while now, Marney. Interest is compounded daily, remember."

Marney tangled her fingers in the red hair of the wig. "All righty, I suppose I can make a token payment right today," she said tentatively. "You gotta be aware that the salary they're payin' me in this hole isn't anywhere near lavish."

Cimarron smiled more broadly and snapped his metal fingers. "Sleeper is willing, if certain conditions are met, to cancel the *entire* debt."

"I'm not going to bed with any more of his ugly friends."

Leaning toward her, resting his silver hand on her slim shoulder, Cimarron told her, "I've got you booked up in Sweetwater, Marney. At $2,500 a week. You'll be playing the lounge at the Sweetwater Casino."

She frowned at his image in her mirror. "Do I have to take off my clothes?"

"No, not at all. This is a high-class situation. Sing, dance, do some shooting. All very tasteful."

"What's the darn catch?"

Cimarron said, "You spent quite a lot of time out in Greater Los Angeles."

"I worked on the vidnet for a couple years, until I—"

"Among your many friends was a private eye named Sid Gomez."

She looked up at him over her shoulder. "He really was a friend. Gomez pulled me out of a heck of a mess once, an' it was just only 'cause he was my friend. Of all the—"

"Gomez, so we hear, is coming to Texas."

"Somehow that doesn't cheer me," she confessed. "No, 'cause it sounds like you got somethin' nasty in mind for him."

"Not at all," Cimarron assured her. "Not at all, Marney. The situation is simply that there are certain people curious as to what he'll be doing once he arrives in the Sweetwater area."

"You want me to spy on him, huh?"

"Let's call it supplying us with information," he said, still smiling. "You do that for a few days, or however long it should take, and then Sleeper will forget completely that you ever borrowed any dough from him."

"And what happens to Gomez?"

"You have my word that no serious harm will befall him."

"But they're gonna do a lot of unserious harm."

The pressure of his metal fingers increased on her shoulder. "Were I you, Pistol Packin' Marney, I'd accept this little assignment," he advised her. "Otherwise I'll probably have to do you serious and substantial harm."

Marney asked, "They won't kill Gomez?"

"If they wanted to kill the guy, they'd just go kill him, wouldn't they?" He shook his head. "What they want, though, is a detailed inside report on what he does and whom he sees while poking around Sweetwater and vicinity. You can provide that. And, by the way, I won't even take the usual agent's fee out of your $2,500."

After almost a full minute, she asked, "When do I go to Sweetwater?"

"Right now," Cimarron answered.

THE SKYCAB SAID, "I never can get used to this GLA weather." The windshield wipers came clicking on as the cab climbed higher into the rainy midday sky. "It's sunny, then it's raining, then it's foggy, then it's smoky, then it's sunny. All in the same blinking day."

In the passenger seat, Jake said, "Aren't you a local cab?"

The voxbox on the dash replied, "Naw, I was built in Outer Detroit four years ago. Michigan, now there's a place for dependable climate. You understand what I'm saying? You get a blizzard and it lasts a week, and it's a blizzard all the way through. Then you get a tornado and it's a plain and simple tornado. Weather there has a beginning, a middle, and an end. As in classical drama. None of this back-and-forth Greater LA crap."

"Interesting," said Jake.

"They shipped me out here a year ago and it's been inconsistency ever since."

"Interesting," said Jake.

"If I'm bending your ear too much, just push that green button on the panel there."

Jake responded, "Just so I get to the Skyport on time, your babble doesn't faze me."

"Going on a vacation, are you?"

"Business trip."

"Where to?"

"Elsewhere."

"None of my beeswax, eh? There, let me tell you, is another difference between out here and back there. Sure, in Michigan just about everybody is open and confiding. 'Where you bound, pal?' 'Why, I'm heading for Singapore to have a wart removed from my backside. Anything else you'd care to know?' Out here, however, maybe because of all the show business going on, everybody is sneaky and secretive. You ask me—oh, boy!"

The cab was suddenly swaying and slewing through the rainswept sky. Then it commenced to drop down through the wet grayness.

"What's going on?" asked Jake.

"I'm losing control of this crate," said the voxbox in a feeble, fading voice. "Somebody's—*awk!*"

Jake unfastened his safety gear and pulled out his stungun.

Glancing down through the see-through plastiglass floor of the rapidly dropping skycab, he saw that they were heading for a landing on a deserted stretch of scrubby beach someplace in the Long Beach Sector.

The skycab landed hard, bounced twice, and ceased to function.

22

I_T was raining hard when they came to take her away. The wind was rubbing and scraping at the windows of Susan's room.

She'd been sitting in the deep armchair, listening to the rain hit at the domed ceiling. Beside the chair rested a lunch tray that held an uneaten soyloaf sandwich, an untasted plazcup of citri-sub, and a cold mug of nearcaf.

Days like today, slow gray days, she didn't like at all.

Well, to be honest, she'd long since lost the capacity to enjoy just about any sort of day.

For a while last night, though, she'd felt almost hopeful.

"Yes, *almost* hopeful," she said aloud. "I guess that pretty much sums up my state of mind."

Being there with Molly and Dan and Dan's father, she'd started to feel that she still did have a chance. She'd be able to straighten out the tangle of her life. Quit Tek for good, lose any need for the comforting illusions the electronic drug created. Equally important, she would find a way to talk to her father, tell him what she was feeling, explain why Juneanne Stackpoole's being in their house was so painful to her.

The talk Susan had had with Jake Cardigan while he flew her home in his skycar had buoyed her up, too. He was outwardly tough and cynical, but she sensed a gentleness and a caring inside. With him for a friend, somebody she could get in touch with if she felt herself slipping, Susan was almost certain she could get herself straightened out.

Cardigan had handled her father, too. He delivered her home and explained she'd simply dropped over to visit with Molly and his son. Made all the trouble with Juneanne seem like an accident and actually calmed her father down. Very few people were able to subdue her father's spells of anger.

What she had to concentrate on was getting out of the slump she was in today. She had to work up the nerve to contact Cardigan and ask him to—

"This will go extremely smoothly and painlessly." Someone, unannounced and uninvited, came into her bedroom.

"Who are you?" She pushed back deeper into the big chair.

The intruder was a tall blond android in a spotless pale yellow suit. He smiled and said, "I'm Alyn—that's A-l-y-n—and I'll be your indoctrinating therapist at—"

"Go away!" she cried. "You're from them. From Stolzer's."

"I work for Dr. Stolzer, yes, that's true," said Alyn, leaning back against the shut door. "You're a very bright and intelligent girl, Susie. I know because I've spent the morning doing my homework on your case. Someone as smart as you are ought to be able to perceive that Dr. Stolzer can, if you'll simply relax and let it happen, clear up all your problems."

"Go away! This is my room. I didn't send for any goddamned nuts-and-bolts medic who—"

"Easy, easy." The android came closer and she noticed a faint medicinal smell.

"Who sent you? My father wouldn't try to drag me back to that hellhole without discussing—"

"Is that a nice thing to say about Dr. Stolzer's establishment, Susie?" Alyn moved nearer. "Is that a kind or thoughtful thing to say about a man who did you such a world of good?"

"If he did me so damned much good, why do I have to go back there?"

"You've slipped, I'm afraid. You've become dangerous, Susie. To yourself, of course, and to those around you who are concerned for you."

"Juneanne. It's that bitch who's trying to ship me off to the loony bin." She stumbled up out of the chair, stood facing the big mechanical man.

"I'm running out of time," he said evenly. "Come down to our comfortable medivan now or—"

"Where's my father? I won't do anything until I can talk to him."

"I'm afraid he's away on business," said Alyn. "He did, however, consult with Dr. Stolzer and give him an unqualified okay before he took off."

"Where's Juneanne?"

"Consulting with her physician at the BevHills Health Management Complex," answered the android. "She suffered serious injuries when you attacked her yesterday, Susie."

"That's not true. She's trying to—"

"You'll have to come along." He reached out for her. "Let Dr. Stolzer help you, Susie."

She tried to run, tried to dodge around him and get at the door.

"I said, come along." Alyn caught her arm. His palm made a tiny clicking sound as a needle shot out and bit into her flesh.

"You can't—"

She lost consciousness all at once.

The android stood back, let her fall to the floor. Then he bent, picked her up, and carried her out into the rain.

THE DISABLED SKYCAB was sitting on the empty stretch of beach with the rain hitting at it.

Jake, stungun in one hand, was working at getting a door open. But both of them were frozen.

". . . back in Detroit," muttered the cab's voxbox. ". . . back in Detroit . . . back in Detroit . . ."

There was no sign of anyone outside in the rain.

About a dozen yards away sat a defunct food stand with a sign reading SOYDOGGIES IN THE SAND dangling from its neowood awning.

All at once both the metal doors went flapping open.

Jake ducked down, staring out at the rain-swept beach.

After a moment, he dived free of the cab. He went out the left-side door and kept the downed vehicle between himself and the food stand.

The rain was heavy and chill. It slammed at him as he crouched down, scanning the stretch of beach.

"Nobody's going to get hurt," called a fluty voice.

The large bald man emerged from the hot dog stand. He held both empty hands out in front of him.

It was the goon Jake had recently identified as Malcolm Summerson.

Jake remained ducked down.

"We have a simple business proposition for you, Cardigan," piped Summerson, moving a few steps closer.

"Outline it to me from there," advised Jake.

"Hey, there are no hard feelings. Even though you fouled me the last time we met," called the big hairless man. "The people I work for have looked into your background, Cardigan, and—"

"That would be the NewTown bunch, huh?"

"Might be, maybe. Anyhow, Cardigan, they found out you were an ex-con with an unsavory reputation. They decided— 'Why not just bribe the guy?' It'll save us all a lot of trouble. Am I right?"

"So you hijacked my cab and landed it here simply so you could offer me a payoff?"

"Exactly," Summerson assured him. "Oh, and also to impress you with our capabilities for tracking you and getting our hands on you if need be."

"And you're alone here? There wouldn't be, say, two or three other louts waiting in that shed with lazguns?"

"I'm by myself. And I'm no lout, Cardigan. During my college years I—"

"Sorry. I'm not interested in a bribe." Jake suddenly stood up and, just as Summerson reached for his shoulder holster, fired his stungun.

The sizzling beam snapped into Summerson's chest and he, making an angry, groaning noise, took two unintended hopping steps backward. Then he hit the beach with a splattering thud and passed into unconsciousness.

Jake had thrown himself to the wet sand as Summerson fell. And when the two husky men came charging out of the stand with drawn lazguns, he was again behind the disabled skycab.

Before they realized that, he shot them both.

23•GOMEz

was whistling quietly, but what he was feeling was uneasy.

The night streets of Sweetwater, Texas, were brightly lit and filled with noise, laughter, and music. The huge litesigns throbbed and glittered in multicolored brilliance, the walkways were crowded with people. The Museum of Western Swing was sending loud, twangy music out into the glaring streets over a dozen large floating voxboxes, the Longhorn Saloon was promising SIMULATED CATTLE STAMPEDE—EVERY HOUR ON THE HALF HOUR!! And the oil well atop the Wildcat Hotel was sending up a continuous simulated gusher.

Gomez had the impression that somewhere in the midst of this festivity there was someone who was watching him. Someone who wasn't especially fond of him.

"Muy loco," he advised himself. "Quit giving yourself the heebie-jeebies, *amigo."*

What he had to concentrate on was his job.

He turned onto the side street he was seeking. There was less light here, less noise, and fewer people.

Just outside the entrance to the Estrella Café stood a battered, chrome-plated robot wearing a dusty Stetson hat. "Spare a few Banx chits for a bot what's fallen from grace, pard?"

"How'd you fall, *pobrecito?"* inquired the curly-haired detective, halting.

"I was once the lead singer in a prominent country and western robot band," began the forlorn mechanism. "One fateful day—"

"Is O'Rian in there?" Gomez asked, leaning closer.

"Who wants him?"

"Sid Gomez."

"Hold on a mite, pard." The robot took off his hat and fiddled with the crown. A faint humming sound commenced in his metal skull and his left eye glowed yellow as he looked Gomez up and down. After thirty seconds, he said, "Go sit in Booth 13, Sid, and consult the astrologer andy there."

"Gracias." Gomez moved on and entered the Estrella.

The café was long and narrow, and the high-domed ceiling offered a view of a star-filled portion of night sky. There were fifteen booths on each side of the place. Some were devoted exclusively to dining, but more of them offered consultations with robot fortune-tellers and android astrologers.

The android in Booth 13 replicated a plump middle-aged woman. She wore a star-studded black robe and a matching turban. Inhaling sharply as Gomez slid in opposite her, she pressed both hands to her bosom. "Ah, I fear that the stars do not favor you, young man."

"Could just be heartburn, *señora*. I want to talk to Zodiac O'Rian."

"Close the booth," she ordered. "I am Madame Futura."

"Catchy name." He touched a toggle on his side of the table and a one-way plastiglass screen slid shut around the booth. "Now, what about O'Rian?"

Madame Futura rested both hands on the tabletop and spread her fingers wide. "You are not especially popular at the moment," she informed him. "Were Zodiac to meet with you in person it might affect his popularity as well. *¿Sabes?*"

Gomez nodded. "So I'm on the shit list in Texas, too?"

"In spades, kiddo."

"Who put me on the list?"

The android held up a forefinger. "You can communicate with him—but keep it brief," she said. Unzipping the front of her robe, she revealed a small viewscreen built into her chest.

A thin, compact man, his face dotted with freckles, scowled at Gomez from out of the screen. "Go back home to Greater LA, pal," he advised. Then he winced, shifted in his chair, and gasped. "Yow!"

"You look to be suffering, Zodiac," observed Gomez. "Is it because you're fretting over my newfound unpopularity hereabouts?"

"That, too," replied the information dealer. "But it's primarily this new spine of mine. I had the old one replaced last month and, I got to tell you, this plyalloy one gives me more aches than the real one did."

"*Qué triste.* Now let me ask you a few questions about—"

"There'll be a new fee system in effect, Sid."

"¿*Sí?*"

"Firstly because I got my new spine to pay for. And secondly, certain people are going to be extremely ticked off with me if they ever find out I supplied you with info."

"How much?"

"A thousand dollars per query answered to your satisfaction."

"*¡Caramba!*"

"Do we deal?" asked O'Rian from the screen in Madame Futura's bosom.

Gomez nodded without much enthusiasm. "Who is it that you're afraid of, Zodiac?"

"Don't know for dead sure, Sid. But it's a team of people who don't much care for you," answered the compact informant. "One of the big NorCal Tek cartels figures in this—and, so I am informed, a large pharmaceutical house in GLA."

"Which cartel?"

O'Rian scratched at the tip of his freckled chin with his thumb knuckle. "It's either the one Zack Excoffon runs out of Marin County—or it might be the Wollter brothers cartel in Frisco. I'm curbing my curiosity in this instance," he explained. "And I don't know which drug outfit, either."

Gomez told the image on the screen, "I want to talk to Avram Moyech."

O'Rian's freckled face took on another pained expression. "That's going to be tricky."

"*Sí,* which is why I'm paying you these outrageous fees, Zodiac."

"Avram, so I hear, is working on a very delicate assignment in these parts," said the informant. "But, let us hope, I may be able to arrange a conversation between you two. It's going to cost you probably $3,000 at least."

"How soon?"

"You're staying at the Sweetwater Ritz, right? I'll contact you there tomorrow morning."

The screen went blank and Madame Futura closed her robe.

THE TALL BLOND ANDROID in the spotless pale yellow suit smiled. "My name is Emlyn. That's spelled E-m-l-y-n."

"You told me your name was Alyn," said Susan Grossman. "Spelled A-l-y-n."

The android chuckled. "Lots of people make that mistake, Susie. Alyn and I look quite a bit alike."

"My name is Susan," she corrected. "Spelled S-u-s-a-n."

"I find Susie more befitting."

After a few seconds the thin, dark-haired girl replied, "You can call me whatever you want, Emlyn. It really doesn't matter."

Her room, a different one from the room she occupied on her last stay at Dr. Stolzer's establishment, was on the highest of the five floors, and the one-way plastiglass ceiling showed a patch of rainy night sky. This room was larger, too, and the walls were a very pale yellow. But not exactly the same shade as Emlyn's spotless suit.

Susan was sitting on the edge of her metal-frame bed, bare feet dangling, wearing a loose-fitting green hospital gown that they'd put on her while she was unconscious.

There were three neowood chairs in the room and the handsome android was sitting in one of them, which he'd pulled over near her bed. "It might be helpful, Susie, if you tell me why you're here."

She answered, "Because that bitch wants to get rid of me."

"Which bitch would this be?"

"The one who had me committed to this shithole."

The android said, "I think you're mistaken about Mrs. Stackpoole's motives," he told her. "She has your best interests at heart, as does your father and—"

"You have the same exact voice as Alyn, too," she pointed out, shaking her head. "Production-line andies. You'd expect a quack like Stolzer to buy top-of-the-line equipment. Considering the prices he charges."

"You're a very hostile young lady."

"Being kidnapped brings out the worst in me."

"You were admitted here at the request of your father."

"And against my will."

Emlyn told her, "That's standard procedure with anyone who's incompetent to make her own rational decisions."

"I want to leave this place now, Emlyn. Will you please allow me to contact my attorney and—"

"You have to *earn* phone privileges, Susie." The blond android crossed his legs, studying her for a few seconds. "Let's talk about some of these delusions you've been suffering from lately."

"I haven't."

"I refer to your strange notion that you saw your late brother being killed."

Susan swung her legs up on the bed and then moved to its other side. "How do you know anything about that?"

Emlyn chuckled again. "The important thing, Susie, is what *you* know," he said. "Will you tell me, please?"

"No, it's no concern of yours or the doctor. I'm not going to tell you a damned thing."

He left his chair, lunged, and reached across the bed. He caught her bare arm and his touch was chill. "On the contrary," he assured her.

24 • HALTing

in the doorway of Bascom's bedroom and clearing his throat, the android valet said, "There seems to be a young woman outside who has our house staked out. She's been there for near to a quarter hour."

The Cosmos chief was just finishing packing the one suitcase he was taking. "And you're just telling me now, Ambrose?"

Rubbing at his temple, the android said, "I'm not one to complain, but I must admit that since my return from the repair shop my mental prowess doesn't seem as tiptop as formerly."

"I'll go take a look. Where is she?" Bascom flipped the case shut.

Ambrose pointed to his left. "On the beach, sitting on a plyoblanket."

Handing the mechanical valet his suitcase, Bascom said, "Stow that in the car. We've got to leave for Skyport by ten A.M."

He slid his stungun out of his shoulder holster and headed downstairs.

From behind the one-way viewindow in the living room he studied the hazy morning beach. "Christ in concrete," he observed, recognizing the slender blond young woman.

Activating the sliding door, Bascom stepped out onto the patio. He kept his gun in his hand but at his side, as he stepped onto the yellow sand. Overhead, high up, gulls circled and squawked.

"I know how you feel." He scowled up into the morning.

"How are you?" asked Kacey, standing up.

"As well as can be expected," answered her father. "Why are you squatting out here?"

"Oh, just keeping an eye on things," she said. "And I was going to pay you a visit eventually."

After he thrust his stungun away, he touched her arm. "I appreciate your concern, Kacey, but I don't need a bodyguard."

"Oh, so? Seems to me that on your own you've managed to get into a substantial mess. If people like me don't take an—"

"Weren't you supposed to be annoying—I mean, working with Jake Cardigan?"

She gave an annoyed head shake. "He seems to have ditched me."

"I'm sure he wouldn't do that, no. He told me he was content with having you as a part-time partner and that—"

"Jake Cardigan has never been content about anything in his whole and entire damned life," said Bascom's daughter. "And having me annoying him and, in his pigheaded opinion, futzing up his investigation isn't likely to cheer him up. Still, I didn't think he'd run out on me completely."

"Oh, he's probably just following up a lead and forgot to let you know." He patted his daughter on the arm.

"And what are you up to, Father? You look, by the way, awfully dejected and downcast."

"Being arrested for murder can have that effect," he explained. "I'm going up to Frisco to nose around."

"Taking your skycar?"

"Nope, using a skyshuttle. Fact is, Ambrose is going to fly me over to the Skyport any minute now. Otherwise, Kacey, I'd enjoy standing out here knee deep in sand and discussing the whole—"

"I'll fly you up to NorCal," she offered. "I happen to be, as I tried to persuade Jake, a damn good investigator. I'd like very much to work with you—and I can look after you, too, so that—"

"No, that wouldn't be fair, Kacey," he cut in as he started back toward his house. "Jake would never forgive me if I split you two up."

"But," she reminded, following him, "I can't locate him."

Bascom stopped and gazed thoughtfully out at the calm morning Pacific. "Maybe I can help you locate him," he said.

FROM HIS IMMENSE top-floor office in the NewTown Pharmaceutical Corporation Building Rowland Burdon could see almost all of NewTown. He found its uniformity depressing this morning and turned away from the viewindow.

"Well?" he said to his computer terminal.

"Still no luck," replied the voxbox.

Rowland crossed to his desk and picked up one of the working models of NPC's newest MoodGun. Rolling up his coat sleeve and then his shirt sleeve, he touched the barrel to his tanned flesh.

The computer said, "Is that wise? After all, Mr. Burdon, that's only a rough approximation of the final product and there are possibly still some bugs in—"

"Shut the hell up," suggested Rowland, "and concentrate on locating my goddamn wayward sister."

"Very well. I was merely—"

"Shut up. Don't say a frigging word until you have some news about Rebecca's whereabouts."

"As you wish."

Rowland studied the mood-choice dial on the gun's stock. "Happiness, joy, euphoria," he muttered, reading the list. "I don't think I can handle euphoria today. No, we'll settle for just plain happy."

After setting the dial, he touched the tip of the barrel to his arm again and squeezed the trigger. A tiny needle came jabbing out. It dug into his flesh and delivered a shot of mood-altering drug into his system. The spot where the needle entered felt cold for nearly a minute.

Rowland replaced the MoodGun on his desktop. "Well, where the hell is Becky?"

"She's not at home, or—"

"Hey, I don't give a shit where she *isn't*. Tell me where she *is*."

The computer replied, "Thus far I've been unable to locate her."

"What about those tailing bugs I had planted in all her skycars and landcars?"

"None are operating. Obviously they've all been disabled."

Rowland rubbed at the needle mark, then rolled down his sleeves. "She must be sneaking off someplace," he said. "Did she take anything with her? Luggage, clothes and the like?"

"I'll check with the household computers," said the computer. "Yes, your sister seems to have taken two small sinleather bags from the bedroom of her beach house in the Laguna Sector. Plus—let me double-check this. Yes, three light summer outfits."

"Shit," said Rowland, "she's heading for the San Peligro Island setup."

"I'll look into that possibility."

Rowland rubbed at his arm again. "Send a memo to Reisberson in Research & Development. Tell that dimwit that the happiness drug in our new MoodGun doesn't work for sour apples," he instructed. "Then tell them to get my tan skyvan ready. I'll be leaving for the Caribbean early this afternoon."

25•DAN

stepped out of the Gunmanship Seminar Room and into the gray academy corridor.

A hand grabbed his upper arm.

"Now what, Molly?" he inquired as she hurried him along the walkway.

"We have to consult with Rex/GK-30."

"Nope, *you* have to. I have to hit the Study Lab and work on my Electronic Forensics CD-paper. Otherwise I'm going to—"

"This is more important. It's about Susan."

"Something happen to her?"

"I think so." Molly tugged him off along a side corridor.

"Explain, huh?"

"I phoned Susan's father this morning—to see how she was doing," said Molly. "He wasn't there and that Mrs. Stackpoole took the call."

"The wicked stepmother."

"She'd like to be, yes. Anyway, Dan, she didn't admit anything outright—but she dropped a few hints."

"And?"

"I got the impression that Susan's not there, isn't at home at all," she told him. "They've sent her someplace else." They'd reached the door of the Background and ID Room and Susan stopped.

"You're afraid she's back with that Dr. Stolzer she was telling us about?"

Molly nodded, tapping on the door softly. "Some terrible place like that," she said. "Rex is going to help us find out exactly where."

THE MORNING SUN was bright in the clear Caribbean sky. It sparkled on the silver-plated guidebot as he led the five tourists and Jake across the stone courtyard of Castle Maldito. Three ancient cannons were installed at one edge of the wide courtyard, aimed out to sea.

"From here, the pirates of old could withstand any assault," the robot was explaining. He gestured at the slanting green hillside and the bright ocean beyond, his yellow straw hat held in his glittering metallic right hand.

"Lot of bunk," remarked the slim teenager who was standing near Jake, shaking her blond head skeptically. "Those look like fake guns to me."

Jake nodded, moving away from the rest of the party.

From the low wall around the stone circle one could see a good part of this side of San Peligro Island. About a half mile below, stretching out between the forest and the white beach was the NewTown Pharmaceuticals facility. It consisted of three low oval-shaped buildings made of plastiglass and neowood. A high metal-strut fence circled the entire setup and there were guardbots at every entrance.

As he stood studying the place, the band of his wrist-phone started to throb, telling him someone was trying to con-tact him.

After glancing, casually, around, Jake crossed the sunbright courtyard and ducked inside the gray stone castle. He trotted up a short staircase and slipped into a small room. There was nothing inside except an ancient-looking chest sitting on the gray floor near one of the high, narrow windows.

Jake stationed himself by a window and activated the phone. "What?"

Karin Tanoshi's thin face materialized on the tiny rectangular screen. "You left a serious mess behind you, Cardigan," she said, anger and disapproval in her reedy voice.

"Nobody's supposed to call me unless—"

"The SoCal Police would like very much to talk to you about that brawl you got into," the Cosmos Detective Agency operative informed him. "It seems, Cardigan, that one of the men you stun-gunned suffered a serious stroke and isn't expected to—"

"Karin, I filed a report, left those louts there, and took off. I had a skyliner to catch," he said evenly. "That's standard procedure for—"

"On top of which, the man you claim was Malcolm Summerson turns out to be a harmless gym instructor from the Oxnard Sector and—"

"When I return, if you're still with the agency, Karin, we'll straighten this out," he said. "Meantime, don't ever call me again." He broke the connection, unstrapped the phone, and jammed it into his jacket pocket.

Apparently Summerson had been able to pull some kind of—

"You okay?"

Jake's hand swung toward his shoulder holster. Then he recognized the figure in the doorway as the skeptical teenager who was sharing the tour with him.

"I'm in tiptop condition," he assured her, letting his gun hand drop to his side but watching the girl closely.

"Old men tend to have all kinds of stuff wrong with them," she said from the doorway. "You came in here and then, when you didn't come out and the rest of them went into another part of the old castle—well, you know, I got sort of worried. But you're all right?"

"Haven't suffered even a mild seizure, but thanks." He stepped into the hallway. "You'd better get back to the group."

"My name's Katrina Bellson."

"Pleased to meet you, Katrina."

"And you're who?"

"Simply an aging tourist." He walked away from her.

THE SAN PELIGRO COUNTRY CLUB also overlooked the Atlantic and the NewTown complex. Its luncheon terrace was floored with simulated mosaic tiles and circled by miniature palm trees set in large crimson tubs. There were about fifty people dining out in the midday sun, all of them protected by the plaz umbrellas that floated over the circular white tables.

Jake was being escorted toward a table by a robot who'd been painted a bright green.

"Hop to it, gov," urged the bot. "His Nibs doesn't like to be kept waiting."

"How come you're green?"

"His Nibs is absolutely dotty over the color. Myself, I find it a bit on the vulgar side."

At a table near the terrace edge sat a very plump man of about sixty. He was wearing a suit of red, yellow, and green flowered material and his white hair and beard were tinted a pale blue. Sharing the table with him was another robot of the exact shape and shade as the one delivering Jake.

"Delighted to see you, old chap," said the plump man as he pointed at an empty chair. "Do sit."

Jake sat. "You're Monte Folkestone?"

"You don't suspect I have a twin, dear boy?"

"Not bloody likely," observed the seated robot.

"Did Sparky introduce himself?" inquired Folkestone.

"Nope. But it—"

"That's Sparky," he said, indicating the standing green bot, "and this is Buddy. Identical twins."

"Very whimsical." Jake rested both elbows on the table. "Walt Bascom contacted you."

"That he did, dear chap." Folkestone reached over to tap Buddy's emerald chest. "Has the promised fee arrived?"

"See for yourself, gov." The left side of the robot's chest snapped open to reveal a compscreen.

Nodding, giving a pleased little laugh, Folkestone said, "Yes, Bascom, the old dear, placed $750 in my Banx account early this morn, just, I imagine, as rosy-fingered dawn was tripping across the—"

"For that sum," cut in Jake, "you're obliged to arrange certain things, Folkestone."

"Do call me Monte, Jake," suggested the plump man. "Since I'm managing your social life while you reside on this blighted island, we must strive to give the impression that we're the closest and dearest of chums, don't you think?"

"Sure, Monte. Now what have you—"

"Go have an intimate chat with our esteemed chef, Sparky, and warn him, in the severest terms, not to make the same mistake with my fish today that he made yesterday," the plump man instructed the standing bot.

"Right you are, gov.'" The robot hurried away.

Folkestone put his hand on Jake's arm and lowered his voice. "Although I am extremely reluctant to admit it, dear boy, I earn a goodly part of my income by arranging social entrée to those who yearn to rise in San Peligro society, such as it is." He took his hand away and stroked his bluish beard. "For you, since you were described as being most eager—the good Lord only knows why— to meet some of the topmost executives at the local NewTown works, I've arranged several introductions and invitations."

"I'm particularly interested in encountering any of them who might be in the need of some extra money, Monte."

"I've already been so informed, dear fellow," said Folkestone. "Tonight you'll be attending a gala party at the mansion of Mrs. Cardwell—a very important local dowager, albeit a certified pain in the bottom. At this soirée, Jake my boy, be sure to strike up acquaintances with Hazel McCay and Theo Kleiner. Both are relatively high up in the NewTown pecking order and both, more's the pity, haven't the faintest notion of how to live anywhere close to within their means." From the breast pocket of his flow-ered suit coat, he fetched a fat realpaper envelope. "An invitation to tonight's festivity you'll find within—along with a list of the other social delights I've set up for you, Jake old man."

Jake accepted the envelope and stood up. "Much obliged, Monte."

"Though it isn't included in the price," Folkestone told him, "you can join me for lunch."

"I'll pass. My social life is too rich and full already." Grinning, he left the plump man and the green robot.

26 • The

air in the long plazwalled corridor smelled convincingly of horses and cattle. Ahead of Gomez, three androids dressed in authentic nineteenth-century cowboy garb were ambling along. One carried a neoleather saddle on his shoulder, while the other carried a lariat in his left hand.

As they neared a door marked ROBOTIC RODEO/MECHANICAL PERSONNEL, the three Stetsoned andies slowed. They stopped, let the seceye scan them, and then entered as soon as the metallic door slid open for them.

Gomez, whistling softly, continued on his way.

A door on his right—ROBOTIC RODEO/HUMAN PERFORMERS— whispered open.

"Well, for darn sakes, if this ain't a coincidence an' a half!" exclaimed the blond young woman who'd emerged and was now smiling at him.

Smiling back, the detective said, "Marney! What causes our paths to cross, *bonita?*"

"It must be, I reckon, fate." Pistol Packin' Marney put both arms around him, gave him an enthusiastic hug, and then kissed him. "Well, sir, that an' my brand-new agent. He booked me to do my act at this here Robotic Rodeo pavillion in the heart of Sweetwater."

"Which act, *chiquita?*"

"Oh, just the trick shootin'," she replied. I quit sheddin' my clothes ages ago."

"*Bueno.* That's a step up the ladder of success."

"A whole lot of steps, Gomez darlin'." Marney stepped back and surveyed him. "I kind of like that cute little potbelly you're developin'. Makes you look even more like a fuzzy teddy bear."

"I have never," he corrected, "remotely resembled a teddy bear or any other sort of stuffed toy. The cut of my jacket gives the illusion that I have a slight paunch."

"What in the heck brings you to Texas?"

"Business. In fact, *cara,* I'd best be moving on. I have to meet somebody in the bowels of this establishment in just—"

"You still with the Cosmos Detective Agency?"

A nearby door, labeled ROBOTIC RODEO/NATIVE AMERICAN ANDROIDS, came sliding open on the left, and two mechanical men in authentic Indian outfits stepped into the corridor.

Gomez waited until they'd moved several yards away before continuing the conversation. "I am, *sí.* And now—"

"Heck almighty, why don't I tag along?" she suggested. "I don't go on for near to two hours yet. I'll stick with you an' then we can grab a bite to—"

"This is a somewhat confidential matter, Marney."

"Darn sakes, Gomez, don't you trust me?" She assumed a hurt and surprised look. "Back in Greater Los Angeles, when you were still a SoCal cop, I helped you out on more than one occasion. Never once did you doubt that I—"

"Okay, all right. You can come along," he conceded. "But you'll have to wait outside while I talk to this *hombre.*"

"I don't mind coolin' my heels."

When Gomez resumed moving along, she took hold of his arm.

He asked, "How long have you had this agent?"

"Oh, not awful long."

A moment later they reached the door marked ROBOTIC RODEO/SIMULATION CONTROL. Gomez halted, faced the seceye, and held up the fake pass Zodiac O'Rian had sent him a short while ago.

The door produced a faint rattling buzz, then slid aside to admit him and the young woman.

"Are you sure now, callin' on Al Lavinsky?" Marney asked.

"*Sí,* but don't ask me any questions concerning—"

"He's very fond of pinchin' the personnel on the fanny," she mentioned. "But after I gave him a demonstration of my shootin' abilities, he lost all interest in my particular backside."

"Guns are a powerful deterrent," observed Gomez. "In fact, it—*momentito!*" He stopped and held out his arm to block her way.

The door to Simulation Control was open, and pale yellowish light was spilling out onto the ramp.

"Wait here, *cara.*" Gomez, sliding out his stungun, eased nearer to the open doorway.

A silver-plated robot sat at a control panel chair, tilted far to the right. The top of his silver skull wasn't there, and a thin spiral of sooty smoke was rising up from within.

Tumbled down on the floor in a twisted sprawl was a fat balding man.

They'd used a lazgun on him and there wasn't much left of his upper back.

Gomez knelt beside the dead man. "This is Lavinsky?"

From the threshold Marney nodded. "They weren't supposed to kill anybody."

"¿Qué dices?" Slowly he stood and took a few steps toward her.

Marney inhaled slowly. "We better hightail it away from here, Gomez," she suggested, letting her breath out in a sigh. "Then we're gonna have to find a nice, quiet spot to have us a little talk."

JAKE ACCEPTED the plazglass of tinted simulated mineral water from the roving robot waiter in the flowered shirt. There were well over a hundred guests out on the dome-enclosed terrace, many of them watching the holographic fireworks display taking place out on the back acre of the Cardwell estate.

Huge multicolored flowers blossomed out in the clear night sky. Then the name Dorothy spread across the blackness in exploding gold-and-crimson letters.

"That's her first name," said a voice just behind him.

"Who? Our hostess?" Turning, Jake found himself facing a tall black woman of about fifty. She was wearing a simple red sinsilk party dress and holding a plazglass of rum punch.

"No, Dorothy Sartain, the gymnast from Portugal. This wingding here tonight is in her honor. Didn't you read your invitation?"

"Not thoroughly enough, apparently."

"You're Jake Cardigan, aren't you?"

"That I am," he admitted. "And you are . . . ?"

She leaned close to him. "Hazel McCay," she said softly.

"One of the people I was hoping to encounter tonight."

"I know. Monte mentioned you wanted to talk to me."

"I do, yeah."

Nodding, Hazel took his free hand and guided him over toward the edge of the enclosed terrace. A five-piece android calypso band was sitting, silent at the moment, on a low dais that was fringed by potted palms.

After they'd stopped near one of the small trees, Jake inquired, "What's your job with NewTown Pharmaceuticals?"

"I'm in Research & Development," answered Hazel, glancing around at the growing party crowd.

"That could be helpful to my cause," Jake told her. "Did Monte—"

"Oh, shit!" She had glanced away and was frowning at two people who were standing at the entrance to the terrace. "There's Rowland Burdon. I didn't know that that nasty son of a bitch was coming to the island. This isn't, Jake, a good time for us to talk. Come see me at my place tomorrow morning early." She gave him her address and moved, unobtrusively but swiftly, away from him.

27 • F<small>OG</small>

was drifting in across the darkening Pacific as Molly guided her skycar through the twilight toward Dan's home.

He was saying, "I don't see that there's much we can do about Susan now. We found out, with Rex's help, that she's been committed to Dr. Stolzer's clinic again, but—"

"We can talk to her darned father—or I can," Molly said, anger sounding in her voice. "I'll suggest that he spring her from that place right away."

"If this Mrs. Stackpoole has as much control of things as Susan says, he won't listen to you."

"No, he'll pay attention," she said. "I'm going to talk to my Uncle Anthony first—he's the one almost honest lawyer in the family—and gather a lot of nice legal phrases I can toss at Mr. Grossman."

"Might work," Dan said.

"I'd like to hear more enthusiasm from the members of the team."

"The problem is, Molly . . . well, Susan's been behaving pretty oddly lately, and I can see where her father'd think she needed some kind of help again."

"So you feel she ought to be locked up in that quack's loony bin?"

"Nope," said Dan. "But you've got to remember that Susan's dad has a much higher opinion of the Stolzer setup than we do."

She punched out a landing pattern on the control dash panel and the skycar began to descend toward the misty beach. "While we were consulting with Rex/GK-30 at the academy, we should've dug some into that Mrs. Stackpoole's background. That might give us some helpful stuff to—"

"I missed two classes as it was."

The car, scattering swirls of night fog, set down next to the condo building.

"I won't come in," said Molly.

"You're ticked off, huh?"

Smiling, she leaned over and kissed him. "Not too much, but I want to get home and start trying to track down my Uncle Anthony. I'll probably have to contact a dozen or so low dives and bistros before running him to ground."

"Whatever you decide to do, I'll back you up." Dan undid his safety gear and opened his door.

"What we're going to do is get Susan out of that place."

He stood on the deck and watched the skycar rise up and then disappear into the thickening mist.

Dan then turned to the sliding door and said, "Open up, it's me."

Nothing happened.

"Open up. Dan Cardigan."

Still nothing.

Reaching out, he touched the door handle. It wasn't locked and he was able to slide the plastiglass panel open.

Very cautiously, Dan took a step across the dark threshold. "Lights," he requested.

The living room remained dark.

Then he heard a faint crackling noise.

An instant later the beam of a stungun hit him in the chest.

MARNEY SPUN GRACEFULLY on her heel and fired the handgun.

The bulky man who'd come charging out of the woods brandishing a flamegun cried out in pain. Staggering, he took three unsteady steps to his right. He fell over and when he hit the simulated yellow grass, his gun hand jerked convulsively. A spurt of flame leaped from the gun barrel, appearing to scorch a wide dark line through the high, dry grass.

"Bingo!" said a voxbox built into the gun.

The fallen body shimmered and disappeared.

"Oaky doaks," said Marney, holstering the gun. "That makes a thousand darn points for me, Gomez darlin'. Looks like I win."

He looked back across the wide stretch of simulated countryside that made up this section of the Sweetwater Shooting Gallery. He slipped his gun into his pocket. "Nobody tailed us here, *chiquita*," he said. "We're *seguro* for now. So let's quit pretending to be customers and have our conversation."

Nodding, she led him over to one of the picnic tables at the edge of the field. She sat down, frowned across the neowood table at him. "Don't be mad at me."

"About what?"

Marney drummed two fingers on the tabletop. "Well, sir," she began, then cleared her throat. "It wasn't, see, any accident my runnin' into you back at the rodeo."

"That possibility had already flitted across my brain. Who put you up to it?"

After she took a careful look around, she answered, "My career hasn't been flowin' along anywhere near as smooth as I let on earlier," she admitted. "Fact is, Gomez darlin', up until quite recent I was doin' my same old strippin' and shootin' act at a succession of dumps and dives all across Texas."

"You having money troubles again?"

"Yep," she said forlornly. "Meanin' I owe some people too darn much money, so they got this feller name of Sam Cimarron to lean on me."

"And he's your new agent?"

"That's him, except he's really just a goon who works for some of the Tek cartels. Anyway, Cimarron told me to come up here an' wait till you showed up."

"They knew I was Sweetwater bound?"

"Surely did."

"What were you supposed to do once you made contact with me?"

"He told me they weren't aimin' to do you any serious harm," she said. "All I was obliged to do was get chummy with you again—and, yep, they did know you an' me was buddies from way back. My job was to tell Cimarron what you was up to and who all you was callin' on."

"He didn't mention what they suspected I was doing?"

"Nope, not at all. But I figure it must sure as heck be somethin' they don't want you to be doin'."

"And you knew I was going to show up at the Robotic Rodeo tonight?"

"Cimarron notified me of that 'bout an hour or more fore you came traipsin' in."

"Did he mention Al Lavinsky?"

"No, he only said you was comin' and for me to get friendly with you awful fast," she replied. "Then I was to start pumpin' you for information."

Gomez looked out across the yellow grass. Far away, two plump women were shooting at a simulated elephant. "Ever hear of an *hombre* named Avram Moyech?"

"Nope."

Gomez took hold of her hand. "Why'd you decide to confide in me, *chiquita?*"

"When I saw Zalinsky dead," Marney said. "I figure that if they'd do him in, they'll more than likely kill you, too. A little lyin' an' informin' I don't mind, special if it helps *me* get out of debt. But I sure as heck don't want to see you get bumped off."

He squeezed her hand, then let go. "Once they realize you're not working for them, they'll add your name to the shit list along with mine."

"Can't be helped. I'm too fond of you to let them kill you, Gomez."

He smiled. "I appreciate your attitude," he told her. *"Bueno.* We've got to con this Cimarron gent, find out where Avram Moyech is holed up. After I've gleaned a few facts from Moyech, you and I will slip, unobtrusively as possible, out of Texas."

"Cimarron more than likely knows where this Avram fellow is," she said.

"I'd bet on that, *cara.*"

"Then you have to get together with Cimarron and find out what he knows."

"An admirable plan," Gomez observed. "Can you help me get it going?"

"Darn sakes," Marney said, laughing, "that'll be easy."

SUSAN WAS SITTING, listlessly, on the bed in her room at the Stolzer establishment. For a while she'd watch, hands folded in her lap, the pale yellow wall opposite. For a while she'd watch the one-way plastiglass ceiling. The night sky overhead was overcast and starless.

Then her eyesight started to blur, her pulse quickened. Pain started blossoming inside her skull and the young woman brought her hands up, pressing her fingertips against her temples. She bent forward, swallowing hard and then murmuring, "I don't want to see anything—nothing—no more."

But another vision hit her. And inside her head she saw Dan Cardigan.

He was lying, sprawled facedown, on the floor of an apartment.

"That's his place," she said, knowing that for certain although she'd never been there.

The hairless man was standing over the body, a grin on his awful face and a gun in his hand.

"They've killed Dan," she gasped, "just the way they killed my brother."

Then she noticed the gun. "It's a stungun," she realized.

So Dan was unconscious, not dead.

Susan saw the hairless man bend and pick up Dan.

"They're taking him someplace."

The big man carried the body toward a doorway.

Susan's body jerked, she began shaking, and the vision shut down and was gone.

She hugged herself, shivering. "Jesus, Jesus—everybody's getting killed or hurt. Anybody who has anything to do with me."

Susan leaped from the bed and ran to the door. She tried the knob, but of course the door was locked.

She began hitting at the metal door with both fists.

"I have to make a call. Got to warn Molly," she cried. "Please, please."

After several minutes a voxbox in the ceiling said, "You must calm down and return to bed, Susie."

It was Emlyn's voice. Or maybe it was Alyn.

"No, but this is important, Emlyn. One of my friends has been hurt and—"

"This is Alyn, dear. Get back to bed."

"They may try to hurt Molly, too. You have to let me phone her. Please."

"You forget, Susie, that you don't have any phone privileges. None at all."

"This is a goddamn emergency, you asshole!"

"If you don't stop this at once, we'll have to come in there and take measures to quiet you, dear."

"Open the damned door!" She started hitting at it again.

And after a while they came in and quieted her down.

28 ● SAM

Cimarron pointed his metal forefinger at Marney. "This isn't much of a spot for a meeting," he said.

"It's got a hell of a lot of privacy," she pointed out to the large black cyborg.

They were in one of the stables in the Robotic Rodeo complex. Twenty robot horses were lined up in neowood stalls on each side of the big structure, and actual horse odors were being pumped in by the aircirc system. The horses had been deactivated for the night and they each stood still and silent. The lights were set on dim.

Cimarron had just come in by way of the door at the far end of the building and was walking toward where Marney stood in

the middle of the neowood plank floor. His metal hand flickered palely in the dim light. "You've made contact with the
greaseball?"

"Hey now, there's no need to call Gomez nasty—"

"Tell me what you have to report." He grasped her wrist with
his metal fingers.

"You're the squeezingest feller I have ever—"

"Give me some information," he urged.

Grimacing, she struggled to get free of him. "Let go of me or
I'm not going to be able to talk straight."

He loosened his grip very slightly, but kept hold of her. "I'm
not especially fond of delay."

"Okay, okay. Gomez is in Sweetwater lookin' for some palooka
named Avram Moyech."

"That we already know."

"How in the dickens am I supposed to know what you know
when you don't confide a darn—*ow.*"

"Less blather, Marney."

She took a deep breath. "He was aimin' to talk to Al Lavinsky,
who works right here at the rodeo," she continued, exhaling. "But
something went wrong and he never got to—"

"All right. So what's his next move?"

"I don't know."

Cimarron leaned closer to her. "If you want to keep in my good
graces, you damn well better find out what he's planning to do
next. And you're going to have to find out damn—"

Cimarron suddenly let go of Marney and pushed her away from
him. He spun around, swinging up his metal hand.

Gomez, who'd slipped out of a nearby stall to come slowly up
behind him, ducked now and made a dive at Cimarron.

The black man had a lazgun built into his middle finger. He

fired it now, but the beam only went sizzling through the air where Gomez no longer was.

The detective tackled the big man around the knees, then brought a fist up into his groin.

"*Yow!*" Cimarron started to move his metal hand up for another shot.

But Gomez slapped a sharp-pronged metal disk against his lower left arm.

Gasping, Cimarron's body began to tremble and jerk.

He slumped back, flat out on the floor and lay stiff with his eyes open wide and staring.

Gomez tapped the disk with his forefinger and untangled himself from the fallen man.

"Darn sakes," commented Marney, "I didn't think he'd hear you tiptoein' up behind him, Gomez darlin'."

"We underestimated the acuity of his hearing, *sí.*" Gomez squatted beside Cimarron. "What I attached to you, Sam, is a trudisk. I'm sure you and the *pendejos* you work with are familiar with them."

"You're . . . a . . . bastard," said Cimarron in a droning voice.

"*Es verdad,*" Gomez agreed. "But right now the disk sees to it that you have to answer each and every one of my queries with an absolutely truthful response."

"Yes," agreed the drugged Cimarron.

"Where's Avram Moyech?"

After a few seconds, Cimarron blurted, "Tekelodeon."

"That's what?"

"Big Tek den," supplied Marney.

Nodding, Gomez asked the drug-controlled man, "Where exactly is Moyech within that joint?"

"In one of the suites in the Exec Wing."

"Which suite?"

"12A."

"Is he guarded?"

"Two human guards. One on the hall, one in the suite with him."

"Any passwords I can use?"

Cimarron answered, "Say *'sibben elf'* to the guardbot at the corridor entrance."

"What are the guards' names?"

"Outside man is Leon and—"

"Trouble coming!" Marney gestured toward the doorway.

Gomez jumped to his feet and turned. *"¡Chihuahua!"*

A tall, lean man with a lazgun in his left hand was coming into the stable. "What the hell'd you do to Sam?"

"Dios, we did nothing," said Gomez. "This poor *hombre* has suffered some kind of seizure."

As the man came running toward them, Marney slipped away and into a stall.

"We were having a polite chitchat," explained Gomez as he casually moved his hand closer to his shoulder holster, "when Señor Cimarron just fell over."

The new arrival stopped beside his fallen colleague.

"How come his eyes are wide open?"

"Must be a symptom of what ails him."

"And I suppose that trudisk you stuck on his arm has nothing to do with—"

"Out of the way, Gomez!" shouted Marney.

There was a slapping sound, followed by a loud snorting.

A huge black stallion came charging out of the stall Marney had ducked into.

Gomez hit the floor, rolled several times, and sat up with his stungun in hand.

The lean man wasn't as fast. The robot horse hit him directly, knocked him to the floor, and then trampled him under his hooves as he went galloping by.

Gomez leaped to his feet, aimed his stungun, and shot the thin man.

He sprinted closer and used the stungun on Cimarron.

Marney popped free of the stall. She poked at the small silver control box she was holding in her hand.

At the other end of the stable, the robot stallion whinnied twice, reared up on his hind legs. He settled down, ceased to function, and was once again silent and unmoving.

"*Gracias.*" Gomez caught Marney's hand. "Soon as we store these *chingados,* we'll pay a call on Avram. We'll have a few hours before these two return from slumberland."

"Soon as they do," observed Marney ruefully, "they're going to want us dead."

29 • The

robot doorman was chrome plated. He wore a multicolored flowered shirt, white trousers, yellow sandals, and a gun belt holding twin stunguns. He dropped his silvery right hand to one of the guns as Jake came striding into the apartment complex lobby out of the hot, sun-bright morning.

"Your business, sir?" he inquired in his deep, slightly echoing voice.

"I'd like to see Hazel McCay," Jake told the bot.

He hadn't intended to come here, but the NewTown Pharmaceuticals R&D exec had failed to show up for their dawn meeting.

Closing his metal fingers around the sinivory handle of the stungun, the doorman asked, "What was that name again, sir?"

"Hazel McCay. She lives in 135."

The robot produced a jumpy humming noise in his broad chest. After a few seconds, he told Jake, "You're mistaken, sir."

"You mean that isn't the apartment number?"

The robot shook his silvery head. "There is no such person residing here."

"This is the Tropicana Villa building, isn't it?"

"It is, sir."

"Then she lives here."

"There is no Hazel McCay living here. There never has been." The doorman lifted his stungun halfway out of its holster. "I believe you've made a mistake."

"She probably doesn't live anywhere now," murmured Jake.

"How's that, sir?"

"I was agreeing that I've made a mistake." Jake took a few steps backward.

"Have a pleasant morning, sir."

"Such is my intention." Jake backed to the plastiglass doors, keeping an eye on the doorman's guns.

As Jake stepped out onto the morning walkway a dark shadow fell across him from above. He dived against the apartment complex front facade, yanked out his stungun, and stared upward.

A cream-colored skycar was drifting down to make a curbside landing.

Jake remained where he was, slightly crouched, gun out.

The car landed, bounced slightly. The driveside door swung open wide. "You're awfully touchy, Jake," said Kacey Bascom, smiling out at him.

Slipping the stungun away, he approached the skycar. "Welcome to San Peligro, a tropical paradise for those who manage to stay alive."

"I'm ticked off at you," Bascom's daughter told him. "You went sneaking out of Greater LA without so much as—"

"Darn." He snapped his fingers and shook his head. "I had intended to inform you about my itinerary and it completely slipped my mind. How'd you locate—"

"I'm a pretty good detective myself," she said. "As I have to keep reminding you. We are supposed to be working together on this business."

Jake rested a hand on the door and leaned forward. "Matter of fact, I could use a little help."

"If you're looking for a way to get inside the NewTown Pharmaceuticals setup unnoticed and undetected," Kacey told him, "I think I can arrange something."

FROM THE VIDPHONE SCREEN, Rex/GK-30 said, "Relax, kiddo. We'll locate the lad."

Molly said, "Something's really wrong."

"Take it easy and fill me in."

She was in the living room of the Cardigan condo and it was a few minutes beyond eight A.M. The morning outside was an overcast pale blue. "I came by to pick him up," she told the academy bot. "There's nobody here and the secsystem is down."

"Hold on a sec," requested Rex. His image was gone from the screen for nearly ten seconds. "We're dealing with some tricky folks, Moll. I just checked out the security computer that handles that building. It doesn't know there's anything wrong there. They used some kind of pretty sophisticated bypass disabler."

"Who?"

"I'll try to find out, but it's going to take me a while."

"I left Dan off here last night—and I guess I was a little nasty to him." Molly's fingers twisted around each other and she rubbed one thumb across the other. "Between then and now somebody grabbed him."

"Listen, if they were going to kill Dan, they'd have done it and left him there," the coppery robot pointed out. "That means he was snatched and taken—"

"But where'd they take him?"

"We'll find out," Rex/GK-30 assured her. "Meantime, you'd best call the cops and—"

"Not yet, no. I want to contact Jake Cardigan first."

"For a SoCal police officer to be," said the bot, "you don't seem to have a great deal of faith in—"

"Most of the SoCal cops don't think highly of Jake. Especially Lieutenant Drexler, who's working on the Bascom—"

"Jake's on the island of San Peligro, down in the sun-drenched Caribbean," cut in Rex. "I just got that by tapping one of the Cosmos Detective Agency computers. Going to require more time to get you a specific vidphone number and address. You might as well come to school while—"

"No, there's somebody else I have to see," she told the robot. "And you're going to help me with that, too."

"Do my best," promised Rex.

THE DARK-HAIRED REBECCA BURDON sat on the terrace of her rented San Peligro villa looking out at the early-morning Atlantic. Far out over the sea a half dozen skyboats were circling and swooping like giant gulls.

A voxbox concealed amid a border of holographic palm trees said, "A Mr. Jean-Paul Berdanier to see you, mum."

She rose up from the high-back neowicker chair, saying, "Send him out here." Turning, she faced the plastiglass doorway.

A moment later it slid silently open and a tall, thin black man in a pale yellow suit stepped out into the bright sunlight. "So very good to see you again, Rebecca dear."

"I have something quite important I want to talk to you about, Jean-Paul." She indicated one of the chairs.

Berdanier seated himself and, carefully, crossed his legs. "You seem distraught and unhappy, dear."

Sitting in the neowicker chair facing his, she said, "Can we talk off the record?"

"Of course, Rebecca," he assured her. "I'm not here in my capacity as Caribbean director of the International Drug Control Agency. I am—and, please, don't ever doubt it—your friend and admirer." He studied her pale face for a few seconds. "Does this have to do with your brother? I know you and he don't always—"

"It does have to do with Rowland."

"A shame you two can't—"

"You know about the SinTek project that NewTown Pharmaceuticals is involved with?"

He chuckled. "I'd better know about it," he replied. "The IDCA is very much interested in a safe electronic drug that has the potential of weaning Tekheads off the real stuff. Is there some snag in the project, dear?"

"No, NewTown will have the testing samples of SinTek ready in two months. Exactly as promised."

"That's very gratifying," said the thin black man. "What then is worrying you?"

Shoulders slightly hunched, she leaned forward in her chair. "SinTek is just a cover."

"A cover, dear?"

"Rowland is in cahoots with a TekLord back in California. Zack Excoffon."

Berdanier straightened in his chair. "That can't be true."

"It is, though. Rowland agreed—for a very handsome amount

of money—to set up a Tek-manufacturing plant for the man," she continued. "It will turn out a very high-grade Tek. Real Tek, not a harmless imitation. And because of the quantity being manufactured, the NewTown Tek will be a lot cheaper to make. Which will mean greater profits for everybody."

Slowly, the drug agent stood. "You're telling me that you and your brother are producing illegal drugs?"

"Yes," she replied. "I have to tell someone. I want this all to stop."

He looked out toward the sea, deep lines forming across his forehead. "It's going on right here on the island, isn't it?"

"Yes, that's right," said Rebecca. "The fact that we're going to be turning out SinTek at this facility will serve as a cover, Rowland figures. Nobody will question the supplies and equipment being brought in. It will look, so he hopes, like everything is being used for the synthetic Tek."

Sitting down again, Berdanier leaned back and sighed. "You've put me—this little conversation of ours has put me, dear, in a very uncomfortable position."

"I know, but I need advice. I need help," she said. "And it isn't only illicit Tek that's involved."

He took her hand. "I'll help you as much as I can, dear."

Very quietly she told him, "They're killing people."

He let go her hand, got up, stared down at her. "What do you mean?"

"Anyone who might cause them trouble, expose what they're up to," she said. "Rowland and Excoffon have already had several people killed. There was a man in SoCal—his name was Rothman or Grossman, something like that. He was killed because he found out something about what the SinTek project was really all about."

The IDCA agent said, "His name was Dwight Grossman. But

Walt Bascom, the head of the Cosmos Detective Agency, is being charged with that death."

"No, they framed Bascom. Excoffon felt it would be clever to get rid of him along with Grossman."

Berdanier moved a few feet away from her. "What do you want me to do, dear?"

"I suppose I'm just about as guilty as my brother. I knew what was going on and I haven't done a damned thing about it."

"You're doing something now."

Rebecca said, "Truth to tell, Jean-Paul, I guess I don't particularly care about myself. I want all this Tek business to stop. If you want to have your IDCA raid the facility here, I can provide you with floor plans, show you the location of the concealed Tek lab and—"

"That won't be necessary, sis." Rowland Burdon came walking across the terrace, smiling at his sister.

Rebecca got up. She said, "Jean-Paul, you can arrest him right now. I'll supply you with—"

"Not likely, dear." Berdanier smiled apologetically.

Rowland told the IDCA man, "You can take off now, J-P. Thanks for alerting me. I've been hunting all over the island for Becky."

"Sorry, my dear." Berdanier nodded at the woman before he hurried away.

30 • H

E woke up shivering. It was very early on a gray, overcast morning and Dan didn't know where he was.

In fact, he wasn't certain who he was or exactly what his name was.

He had awakened in this long, chill room a few minutes ago and very soon realized that he no longer had any clear idea about his identity.

He'd almost come up with a name for himself. Dan something . . . but it had faded swiftly away and he couldn't retrieve it.

He was sitting on the edge of a gray cot, hunched, fists clenched, and struggling to remember. Who he was, where he came from, how he got here. Anything.

There were exactly twenty cots in the neowood room, in two rows of ten each. All the others were occupied by sleeping young men.

Out beyond the plastiglass windows were at least a dozen other long, low buildings. A wide dirt roadway ran through the two rows of buildings and all around stretched dense, shadowy woodlands.

His left arm was aching. Rolling up the sleeve of the faded blue work shirt he found himself wearing, he saw three inflamed needle marks on his upper arm.

"Might as well get dressed, Hank. Wake-up's going to sound any minute now."

He looked to his left. A lanky black young man of about seventeen was getting up out of the cot next to his. "You talking to me?"

"You're Hank, aren't you, cousin?"

"I don't know." He frowned, rubbing his fingers up and down over his forehead. "I don't think so."

The young man got into a pair of work trousers. "That's what they told us your tag was when they dumped you here last night."

"Told you my name was Hank?"

"Yep, Hank Weiner. Where'd they transfer you from?"

The question didn't mean anything to him. He asked, "What shape was I in when I arrived?"

"Out cold, which is the way a lot of the new recruits check in." Dropping to the cot edge, he started tugging on his neoleather boots. "I'm Ogden Whitney."

"Ogden. Hi." He noticed he had a pair of work boots of his own sitting on the plank floor beside his cot. "I'm sorry . . . but I just don't seem to have any recollection of how I got here or where I came from."

Ogden zipped up the front of his faded blue work shirt. "More than likely, cousin, you been wiped."

"What do you mean—a brainwipe?"

"They're not supposed to do it." Ogden started to make his bed. Other young men were rising, getting dressed. "But with some of the tougher recruits they—"

"What the hell am I a recruit in, Ogden? Is this some kind of militia or—"

The young black man laughed, rubbing a knuckle under his nose. "You're now an official resident of Junior Workers of America, Camp 30."

He'd heard something about the Junior Workers of America. "Wait now," he said. "This is some kind of detention station for juvenile criminals, isn't it?"

Ogden laughed again. "Isn't that what you are, Hank?" he inquired. "You got to be what they call a juvenile offender or you can't participate in the JWA. And you got to be a pretty nasty mean-ass one to get stuck here in 30."

Hank shook his head. "I don't know—I guess maybe I am."

"The basic philosophy of JWA is that they never make mistakes," explained Ogden. "You're here, you're bad. The system is never wrong."

"It's just that—listen, I can't remember anything." He gestured at the cot. "Not a damn thing before I woke up this morning."

"Mindwipe for sure, cousin."

"Where exactly is this camp?" Hank asked him.

"Mississippi Territory." Ogden came over and stood close to him. "You got any idea where you were before?"

After a few seconds, he answered, "No."

Ogden put a hand on Hank's shoulder. "I'll try to help you out much as I can, cousin," he told him. "You seem like your brains are more futzed up than just about anybody else here. And that's saying something."

A loud, shrill hooting commenced blaring out of the voxboxes up in the rafters.

Hank flinched. "What the hell is that?"

"Wake-up," answered Ogden. "Time to rise and shine and greet a new day at 30, cousin."

SIDE BY SIDE, Jake and Kacey walked along the glaring white beach. The morning sea was a deep crystal blue and it came rushing in at them across the wet sand.

A silvery robot in a floral shirt and realstraw hat came walking from the opposite direction. He was pushing an ebony portable bar. "Tropical drinks, mister and lady? Legal drugs? Tour maps?"

"None of those," Jake told him.

"You're not enjoying San Peligro to the fullest," observed the bot, rolling on.

"I've noticed that."

After a moment Kacey pointed skyward. "There. See?"

Flying low overhead was a lemon yellow skyvan with the word FOODZ printed in large magenta letters on its belly and side.

"How often do they bring in the meals for the NewTown cafeterias?"

"Twice a day," she answered. "This time every morning, again at three in the afternoon."

"And your contact at Foodz is?"

"A very loyal supporter of J. J. Bracken."

"I don't know if I trust a political loon."

"His name is Edwin Temmerson and he heads up the whole Foodz operation in the Caribbean area," she said, nose wrinkling. "We can trust him."

Uphill on their right sat the NewTown Pharmaceuticals complex, the trio of squat plastiglass-and-neowood buildings protected by the glaring metal fence. Gunmetal robots, five of them on the beachfront side, stood at intervals along the fencing.

"Is this Temmerson guy fond enough of your boss to go up against the Burdons?"

"I'd say yes," she said, "especially after I con him into believing he'll be helping J.J. by helping me. And if, which I doubt, he won't let us slip inside by way of one of his delivery vans, he'll at least help me get detailed maps of the interior of the whole NewTown setup here."

"I already have those," Jake informed her.

"Well, I'm having lunch with Edwin today. I'll work out—"

"Do it deftly and subtly, huh? Otherwise he's liable to warn the Burdon twins that we—"

"Jake, sooner or later you're going to have to accept the fact that I am not a nitwit." She halted on the warm sand and stood looking toward the NewTown buildings.

A light wind was coming across the sand from the sea, and the fronds of the palm trees that rose up behind the drug plant were flickering.

Taking hold of her arm, Jake headed them back the way they'd come. "Couple of those guardbots are commencing to eye us."

"You're overcautious."

"Helps in my work."

31 • THE

reception room of Dr. Stolzer's establishment had a strong metallic smell. Each pale green wall held a small, noncommittal landscape painting. The aircirc system kept the temperature just below the comfort level.

When the tall blond android in the spotless pale yellow suit came into the room, Molly Fine stood up and smiled. She was wearing a skirtsuit that made her, she hoped, look two or three years older.

"Miss Eshler?" inquired the andy.

"Xena Eshler, from the Young Adult Psychiatric Overlook Committee of Greater Los Angeles." She produced the very convincing fake ID packet that Rex/GK-30 had provided her with.

"I'm Evelyn. That's E-v-e-l-y-n." He took the identification materials and, frowning, sifted, slowly, through them. "These all seem in order, Miss Eshler. What do you require of us?"

"You'll find this in order, too." Molly handed him the spurious but nearly foolproof court order. She'd had to rely on a fake order because her attorney uncle, the nearly honest one, had informed her last evening that it would take him at least four days, if not more, to arrange for a real one.

Evelyn's very plausible pink forehead furrowed. "Miss Grossman is not supposed to have visitors," he said. "None at all at this stage of her therapy."

"Obviously Judge Maxon doesn't agree. She feels that the YAPOC/GLA needs to clear up at once, and as soon as possible, the charges of malpractice and mistreatment that have arisen concerning Miss Grossman."

"What charges?"

"Here's a copy." Another expert fake document was passed from Molly to the mechanical man.

After a moment of scanning it, Evelyn said, "Dr. Stolzer is out of the country at the moment. I've been left in charge." His sigh was very believable. "Very well, Miss Eshler. We don't want any trouble. Although I can assure you Miss Grossman, as all our patients, is being very well treated." Turning his back, he went walking across the chill reception room toward a black door.

Molly followed.

As they stepped into a long, cool corridor that smelled of metal and medications, the blond android told her, glancing back over his broad shoulder, "You're aware that this particular patient is seriously ill. That she also suffers from delusions. Most of what she says, therefore, is little more than that fantasy of a very disturbed young woman."

"I've dealt with a great many patients of this sort."

"You are, I might mention, quite young yourself and I wonder if—"

"My organization feels that youth best understands youth."

"Not a theory I subscribe to myself, but I acknowledge their right to hold it."

They went through another doorway, along another corridor. At its end, Evelyn touched his palm to an ID plate. The door recognized his whorl pattern and rattled open.

Evelyn moved along the new corridor they'd entered, stopped at a door, and pressed his hand to another ID plate. This door opened more quietly and he started across the threshold.

"I have to see her alone," said Molly, not following him.

Evelyn came back into the hall. "That could be dangerous to—"

"You apparently didn't read the court order as thoroughly as you should've, Evelyn."

"I'll give you ten minutes." Stepping aside, he gestured for her to enter Susan's room.

Molly did that. She put her finger to her lips as Susan looked up from her bed, about to speak.

The door slid shut behind her. Molly put her finger to her lips again.

Then from a pocket in her jacket she took a bug-disabling disk and stuck it to the nearest wall.

"It'll take them a few minutes to realize they're not getting a darn thing from their eavesdropping gadgets."

Susan left the bed, ran over to Molly, and hugged her. "I'm glad you're not dead."

"What do you mean?"

"I saw—I had another vision. This was about Dan."

Molly took hold of both her friend's arms. "He's not dead?"

"No, I don't think so. But the bald man—the one you saw at the

Tek joint—he stungunned Dan last night and took him away from his apartment."

"Do you know where they took him?"

Susan shook her head. "No, I didn't see that."

Molly said, "I knew Dan was missing and I've been trying to find him. No luck so far, though. What you saw should help. Now—what about you?"

"That bitch—she had me stuck here."

"I'm working with one of my lawyer uncles to try to get you clear of this place," she said. "But it may take a few more days. I faked my way in today so I could see how you were. What's wrong?"

Susan went backing away from her. She started to shiver violently. "It's . . . another . . ." She stumbled, sat on the edge of her bed.

"Another vision?"

Susan doubled over, arms pressing into the stomach. "They're using stunrods on him . . . hurting him," she gasped.

"Dan? You're seeing Dan?"

"Yes, he's at—"

"What are you up to, Miss Eshler?" The door had snapped aside and Evelyn was back in the room. "Why have you blanked our surveillance system?"

THERE WERE NO WINDOWS in any of the rooms. But the wallscreen in the stark black-and-white parlor provided a view of a stretch of San Peligro beach and ocean. It was a looped view that took four minutes and thirty-seven seconds to unfold. The same palm trees fluttered in the same way in the same gentle ocean breeze, the same five gulls swirled and dived through the glaring sky, the same stray dog barked silently at the same beached crab.

Rebecca Burdon left her hard white armchair, began pacing aimlessly on the black carpeting.

The white door whisked open and her brother stepped in. "Comfy, Sis?"

"Even for a fool like you, Rowland, this is excessive," she told him. "Locking me up in the innards of this NewTown facility— once I get out of here, I'm going to my attorneys."

Perching on the arm of a white sofa, he smiled. "You came here voluntarily," he informed her. "I'll testify to that. And so will several of our top executives. People who witnessed your unfortunate breakdown in the Exec Dining Room this morning at breakfast." He shook his head, sighing. "Sad, but then you've always been exceptionally high strung."

"I've had a nervous breakdown, have I?"

"Long ago, Becky, I should have realized that you were hopelessly addicted to several illegal drugs, both electronic and old fashioned. My fault, really, for not noticing sooner."

"How long do you expect to get away with an idiotic story like that? My attorneys will eventually—"

"They've already been notified of your condition," he said, smiling again. "As to how long you're going to be a guest on the island—not long at all."

"You can't kill me, Rollo, without risking—"

"One of the symptoms of your unfortunate condition is an exaggerated feeling of persecution." Rowland stood. "There's absolutely no need to kill you, Sis."

"What then?"

"I intend to go ahead with our Tek venture," he said evenly. "You tried to betray me to the International Drug Control Agency. Good thing Jean-Paul has been working for me for nearly a

year. That's one of the main reasons we set up the clandestine
Tek plant here."

"I went along with the Tek idea, which was wrong and stupid.
But killing people is—"

"Once that Dr. Stolzer works with you, you'll feel differently,"
promised her brother. "You'll be, for the first time in many a long
year, happy and cooperative."

She glared at him. "You're not going to let that quack
touch me?"

"Come, Becky, Stolzer's highly respected," said Rowland.
"And once he gets through modifying your brain, you'll agree that
he's a wonderful fellow."

32 • T_{HE}

huge gunmetal guardbot blinked, which produced a metallic clacking sound. He scratched at his side with dark metal fingers, then rubbed his palm across his domed skull, then poked Gomez in the breastbone. "Say that again, *amigo*," he requested.

"*Chihuahua*," remarked Gomez, "a Mexican bot. *¿Qué pasa, hombre?*"

"Spare me the greaser lingo, Shorty," requested the robot who was guarding the exec wing corridor deep inside the Tekelodeon complex. "Just simply repeat what you just now said to me."

Gomez said, "*Sibben elf.*"

"So?"

After giving a perplexed look to Marney, who was standing a few feet behind him, Gomez leaned closer to the mechanical man. "It's the password, *cabrón.*"

The gunmetal head rattled slightly when the bot shook it. "It *was* the password, *pato,*" he told him. "Yesterday."

"Oops," observed Gomez.

The guardbot's arm, the one with the lazgun built in, started to swing up.

"Darn sakes, we got no more time for arguin'." Marney whipped out a stungun and fired.

"Madre de Dios," exclaimed the robot, going up on tiptoe for a few seconds before starting to topple over.

Gomez caught him, bicycling back as the full weight of the guardbot hit him. "This isn't, *chiquita,* the stealthy entry into Moyech's lair that I had in mind."

"Stack him over yonder, darlin'," Marney suggested. "Then let's get movin'."

JAKE WAS ALONE in his hotel room when the call came.

"Molly Fine calling," announced the vidphone.

"Put her on." Jake crossed to sit down in front of the phonescreen.

A very pale and agitated Molly popped up. "Jake, Dan's in trouble. I should have called you earlier except I thought it was best to—"

"Whoa now," he advised. "Tell me what's happened to him."

Molly took a breath, brought a plyochief up to her nose. "It happened last night sometime, but I didn't find out about it until this morning," she began. "Dan was snatched out of your condo. By that bald man."

"Summerson," said Jake. "Any idea where Dan was taken?"

She gave a vigorous nod. "Yes, I got that from Sue Grossman."

"We're talking about an extrasensory vision?"

"Initially, but I checked it out—as best I could, Jake."

"Go ahead."

"Susan saw Dan at a place called Junior Workers of America Camp 30."

"Jesus, those camps are pestholes. Where's that one located?"

"Thirty is in the town of McClennan, Mississippi."

"Do you have any evidence that Dan is actually—"

"Yes, Rex/GK-30 helped me on this," she answered. "Very early this morning a young man named Henry Weiner arrived at 30. He answers Dan's description—I'm near certain it's him."

"Damn it. They've probably mindwiped him."

"I can meet you in McClennan and—"

"No, I'll take care of this."

"You're sure you—"

"I'm sure," he told her. "How'd you get this information from Susan?"

"It was very tough doing," Molly said. "They tossed her in Dr. Stolzer's setup and I had to fake my way in. I wanted to check on how she was doing, and while I was there—well, she had another vision. But before she could finish telling me about it, one of the goddamned android medics burst in on us." She shrugged her left shoulder. "I sort of had to stungun the lout so I could get all the information from Sue."

"You're doing terrific work, Molly," he said. "I assume one of your lawyer uncles is going to be able to keep you out of the pokey."

"Don't worry about that."

"Where's Susan now?"

"She seems to have left there while the andy was out of commission," she answered. "My uncle tells me not to admit I know where she is. But if she sees anything else, I'll contact you." She leaned forward. "You will get Dan out of that damn work camp, won't you?"

"I will, yeah," he assured her, and ended the call.

AVRAM MOYECH was neither tall nor thin. Standing now in the center of the scarlet room, his bare feet flexing on the thick scarlet carpeting, wearing a short, black sinsilk robe, he measured under five feet four and weighed something over two hundred pounds.

The tall blonde in the neoleather slax and halter was saying, "Of course you're handsome, Av. Gorgeous, to tell the truth."

"You mean that, Francesca?"

"I could never lie to you, darling." Smiling, she took one more step closer to him.

The scarlet drapes covering the high, narrow bedroom windows fluttered gently in a faint night breeze. The five globes of light floating up near the scarlet ceiling glowed a pale scarlet.

"In college, out in Greater Los Angeles," the chubby, bearded man told her, "I had the idea you didn't much like me."

"Ten years ago that was, Av dear." She ran her fingers through his long blond hair, ruffling it, and moved slowly nearer and nearer. "I'm older, wiser. I appreciate you for what you are."

"You told Sam Hollis you thought I was a schmuck. A fat little schmuck."

"Obviously I don't think that now, darling." Francesca stopped quite near to him. Her smile deepened as she put her hands on his pudgy shoulders and pulled him to her. "And we've got all night for me to prove it to you."

"Back to reality, *pobrecito.*" Gomez was standing beside the blonde.

She grimaced, let go of Moyech, vanished. So did the scarlet bedroom.

Moyech shook his head from side to side, blinking. "How the hell did you get into—"

"I'm notorious for invading Tekheads' dreams," explained the detective. He held the Tek gear he'd just yanked from the fat man's head.

Moyech, fully clothed, was sitting on a circular airbed. "Who the hell are you? How did you—"

"Actually, *mierdita*, I'm the one who asks the questions." His stungun suddenly appeared in his hand. He fired it at Moyech.

The man's left hand swung out at his side, the fingers spread themselves wide and then closed into a fist as he passed out and fell back onto the bed.

Gomez hefted up the stungunned Moyech, managed to get him tossed over his shoulder. "*Ai,*" he remarked, "this guy is *muy grueso.*"

Marney, who was across the bedroom, yanked open a door. "Let's us skidaddle, darlin'," she suggested. "We got to vacate this joint real quick."

"Lugging a two-hundred-fifty-pound technical expert around slows a feller down, *cara.*" As best he could, he made it over to the doorway.

They stepped into a dimlit corridor. "If I recall rightly, from the research I did before we invaded the Tekelodeon, this passway'll lead us to where we can sneak out into—"

"Trouble."

A thickset gray-haired human guard had come around a bend about thirty feet down corridor. He reached for the lazgun in his belt holster.

But Marney was quite a bit faster. She snapped out a stungun, fired it, and hit the man in the midsection before he had his gun out of its holster. "Darn sakes, my shootin' has been top-notch this evenin'," she said, grinning. "This current lunkhead yonder makes my score three human beings, one bot, and one android so far."

"Let's haul Moyech someplace where I can question the guy."

"And let's get *me* somewheres where nobody can kill me grave-yard dead."

33 • JAKE's

skycar, picking up speed, climbed up into the bright late-morning sky, circled out over the sea, and then headed toward the southern United States.

Once he'd punched out a flight pattern for Mississippi, Jake activated the vidphone. He used Walt Bascom's private agency number and in under a minute the Cosmos Detective Agency phone system had rerouted the call to the chief at a NorCal number.

Bascom appeared on the small rectangular screen. He eyed Jake, frowned, and asked, "Something wrong?"

"Dan's missing. I'm taking time off to find him."

"Give me some details?"

Jake provided a concise account of what he knew and what he suspected. He concluded with, "I've been working on getting inside the San Peligro NewTown plant on the sly. Trouble's been, the first person who was set to help me has ceased to exist."

"These are very rough folks we're up against."

"When I get back I'll—"

"Your son comes first," said the agency head. "Do you really feel you can put much faith in the Grossman girl? Seems to me, this kind of bunk is about one step above Tarot cards when—"

"I trust her, yeah. I can't explain what Susan Grossman does, but it seems to work."

Bascom inquired, "Did my daughter show up down there?"

"She did. I assume you're the one who sicced Kacey on me."

"Well, I might've provided her with a few helpful hints, extolled the wonderful weather in the Caribbean and so on," admitted his boss. "It was either that, Jake, or have her tag along with me up here to Frisco."

Nodding, Jake asked him, "What are you finding out up there?"

"That Zack Excoffon, noted Teklord, is one of the lads behind the murder frame-up. I've got a lead on somebody inside his organization who's willing to talk—for a hefty fee. Another day or so and I'll know."

Jake asked, "Has anybody contacted the agency about Dan? Asking for ransom, warning us to lay off the case, wanting to contact me and make some kind of deal?"

"Not so far, Jake. And I got a report from your chum Roy Anselmo less than an hour ago," said Bascom. "Nobody's contacted you, I take it?"

"Nope, I checked with my condo and no messages about Dan have come in," he said. "I figure they took Dan to keep him from poking around into the Susan Grossman end of things. Which may mean that Molly Fine's in danger, too. Better put a watch on her."

"Soon as we quit chatting."

"Any news from Gomez?"

"Still in Sweetwater on the trail of the genius who rigged those very convincing sectapes of my debut as a crazed killer."

"I'm going to get Dan out of that camp," he said quietly. "And it probably won't be through legal channels, Walt."

"I'll get you the names of some Mississippi locals who should be able to lend a hand in various ways, legal and otherwise," Bascom promised. "Take me about an hour. I'll call you back."

"Thanks."

"Is Kacey still on the island?"

"Far as I know. I'll be calling her next."

Bascom shook his head. "She's liable to walk into trouble."

"She's pretty capable. Hard to take, but capable."

"I'll see if I can provide some local backup for her so she won't know about it whilst you're away."

Nodding, Jake ended the call. He punched out a new number.

"Where are you?" was the first thing Kacey asked after her image materialized on the phonescreen. "Up in a skycar it looks like," she guessed, head tilted to the right. "So you're sneaking away from me again, huh?"

"If I were sneaking away, I sure as hell wouldn't call you to announce the fact."

"There's something wrong. You look very upset," the young woman said. "What is it? Has something happened to my father?"

Jake replied, "My son's been snatched. I think I know where they've taken him and I'm going there. It means postponing the island part of the investigation for a day or so."

"Jake, that's terrible. Where are you heading? I can meet you there and help you."

"Nope," he told her. "Thanks, but this has nothing to do with you. I'll handle it, Kacey."

Slowly, reluctantly, she said, "Okay. I'll keep working things here."

"Fine, but don't go trying to solo—these guys are extremely nasty."

"Oh, so it's perfectly okay for you to go off and play one-man army, but I'm not qualified to—"

"It's just that I'd hate to see you get killed."

"Meaning you have some feeling for me?"

"Your dad would be annoyed with me if somebody knocked you off," he explained.

She said, "You're an absolute—"

Jake ended the call.

THE PALE BLUE SKYVAN had TexMex Catering emblazoned on its side in golden letters. Gomez, hunched in the pilot seat, was flying it through the dusk in the general direction of Mexico. "Once we arrive in the land of my ancestors, *cara*," he was saying, "I can arrange to have Señor Moyech shipped, very unobtrusively, up to Greater LA and into the arms of the Cosmos Detective Agency. From whence he'll be handed over to the minions of law and order. They in turn will persuade him to repeat the story he told me about rigging the Bascom sectapes. Of course, the cops probably won't use a trudisk, but they'll be able to persuade him to babble a bit."

Marney was sitting next to him, the fingers of her left hand drumming on the control dash. With her right hand she was fiddling with the security screen scanners. "What's that, Gomez darlin'?"

"I've been outlining my brilliant plan for transporting

Moyech—who slumbers back in Pantry 2 on this crate—from
Texas to SoCal by way of Mexico. What's preoccupying you?"

"Well, sir, I'm sort of jumpy." She nodded at the screen. "I
been checkin' up on whether anybody's tailin' us."

"*Sí,* and?"

"No sign of anybody doggin' us."

He glanced at the small screen. "It appears we are as free as a
pajaro."

"Sam Cimarron and those lunkheads he works for aren't goin'
to be very happy with my conduct in this business."

"Once I get Moyech safely delivered," he reminded her, "I'll
arrange for you to be installed in a safe spot."

"We haven't delivered him yet."

"We're moving closer to our goal. It won't—"

"Darn sakes!"

"*¿Qué?*"

She touched the screen. "Two big black skyvans are comin' up
on our tail."

34 • A

As Jake's skycar began to descend toward the landing area behind the large domed house he sought on the outskirts of Yazoo, Mississippi, the dash voxbox spoke. "Switch to a circling pattern. Do not attempt to land yet or you'll be fired upon."

"I've got an appointment with Attorney Krishovnik," said Jake.

"Continue to circle and identify yourself."

"Jake Cardigan, Cosmos Detective Agency. Walt Bascom arranged for—"

"Set down in Landing Section 2. Do not attempt to leave your craft until instructed to do so."

Jake brought his skycar down and waited.

After a moment the voxbox instructed him, "Step clear of your car. Walk to the gate designated X3 and wait there."

"Do all of Krishovnik's clients have to go through this sort of stuff?"

"Attorney Krishovnik has a rare talent for rubbing people the wrong way. Hence he's found it necessary to live a secluded and secure life most of the time. Now move to X3."

Jake did that, stopping on a small yellow rectangle labeled STAND HERE—OR RISK BEING SHOT!

Finally he said, "I'm here to see Krishovnik."

"Lean closer to the gate," said the voxbox in the high neostone wall. "You'll now have your ret patterns scanned."

After his eyes were checked, he was required to press his palm against an ID plate.

"Everything checks out."

Clicking once, the gate swung open inward.

Jake entered a large circular patio paved with simulated flagstones. Across it was another neostone wall and a door labeled GUEST CLEARANCE.

The door slid slowly open and a metallic voice invited, "Step in here, Mr. Cardigan, if you please."

The room beyond the door was furnished like a parlor. There were two white enameled medibots seated in it, each in a striped armchair.

One of the bots said, "Do you object to a blood test? To further confirm your identity, sir."

"Matter of fact, I do," replied Jake. "Tell Krishovnik I'll find a lawyer on my own and—"

"Hotheaded, as advertised." A large frizzy-haired man of about fifty had entered through a side door. He wore a polka dot sinsilk robe and the part of his broad chest that showed was thick with fuzzy grayish hair. "You should've learned by now, *tovarich*, that your fiery temper doesn't gain you anything. Except extended stays in prisons like the Freezer."

Jake eyed him. "Walt Bascom recommended you," he said. "I sure as hell can't see why."

"It's because I happen to be the best—as well as the sneakiest—lawyer in all of the South," said the big man. "Now, sit yourself in one of these chairs and we'll have a discussion of your problem."

"It could be that I don't want to talk to you."

"Don't be a ninny, *kapusta*. Nobody else is going to be able to help you spring your wayward son from that work camp."

"And you can do it legally?"

Krishovnik laughed. "There is no legal way to do it, Cardigan," he informed him. "But there are several really terrific illegal ones. Sit down."

Jake sat down.

WHILE ONE of the pursuing black skyvans remained above and behind the craft Gomez was piloting, the other dropped altitude and sped up.

"How tricky a flier are you, Gomez darlin'?" asked Marney as she unhooked her safety gear.

"Extremely tricky," he assured her. "Why do you ask?"

She tapped the screen. "This here van's aimin' to come in underneath us and the other one's probably goin' to attack from above."

He consulted the screen. "Appears very likely, *sí.*"

"So if you can do a wide backward loop—I think I can take care of both of 'em."

"Alas, *chiquita*, this delivery van we're using in our daredevil escape doesn't come equipped with built-in guns."

"Darn sakes, that's not a problem." She hurried across the cabin to yank open the door of one of the storerooms. "You're forgettin' that I brought most of my collection of guns along with me. I got a couple of powerful lazrifles that'll do the job."

"*¡Chihuahua!*" The low skyvan was firing at them with its lazcannon, and the upward loop Gomez went into took them out of range only a few seconds before the crackling orange beam went sizzling by.

Marney dived into the storeroom, rushing out a moment later hefting two lazrifles. She carried them to a small round window and opened it a few inches. "Do a wider loop now, darlin', and shift us a mite to the left."

"*Bueno.*" He started the maneuver.

Their skyvan went climbing up through the darkening sky. At the top of the loop they were flying upside down.

Marney thrust a rifle barrel through the opening, aimed, and fired.

The crimson beam knifed downward and hit the plastiglass window of the black van beneath them.

The window was sliced in half and came popping out.

Marney fired again, this time into the control cabin.

Considerable sooty smoke came swirling out after a moment. The van commenced wobbling and shimmying. It dropped, rapidly, down toward the ground below.

She laughed. "Got 'em good and proper."

Their skyvan continued its loop and she tried two more shots with the lazrifle.

This time she hit the other pursuing black van, once in its side, slicing a door up, and the second time cutting a large rut in the underside of the engine compartment.

The lazcannon the van had aimed at them went astray. The craft went into a spiraling plummet.

"Bingo," said Marney with satisfaction.

She withdrew the rifle, shut the window, and returned the weapons to the storeroom.

"Should you ever need a testimonial to your abilities as a shooting whiz," offered Gomez, "call upon me, Marney. And now—on to Mexico."

35 • FROM

the wide curving viewindow of the living room in Rowland Burdon's villa you could see a good part of the island. Night was closing in, sweeping across the beaches and filling the jungles. Lights were blossoming in the houses, hotels, and condos. All the lights in the NewTown facility just downhill came on at once and the complex seemed to come bursting out of the darkness.

Reaching into the pocket of his jacket, Burdon slid out a model of NewTown Pharmaceuticals' newest Mood Mist Dispenser. "Very depressing night," he observed as he inserted the plaz barrel between his teeth.

A touch of the trigger squirted a cold-feeling swirl of spray. For a few ensuing seconds his mouth and tongue felt fuzzy.

He swallowed a few times. "We'll have to improve this damned delivery system." Burdon crossed to the Entertainment Sector of the large room. "And the spray sure hasn't pepped up my spirits one hell of a lot."

After settling in one of the low armchairs that ringed the holostage, he picked up the voxselector. "Shakespeare," he said into it.

"Very well, sir."

The wide circular stage began to glow faintly.

A princely figure, life size, materialized. "O! that this too too solid flesh would melt," he said, "thaw, and resolve itself into a dew. Or that the Everlasting had not fixed his—"

"*Hamlet,*" realized Burdon. "Too gloomy. Let's try something else."

The stage emptied.

Then a bearded old man in regal dress showed up. "I am a very foolish, fond old man," he intoned in a quavery voice. "Fourscore and upward, not an hour more or—"

"What's this, *King Lear?* That's your idea of cheerful?"

The king faded away.

A trio of gnarled witches replaced him. One cackled, "When shall we three meet again, in thunder, lightning, or in rain?"

"Get them out of here," ordered Burdon.

He turned out also not to be in the mood for *The Merchant of Venice, Twelfth Night,* or *Othello.*

Then a tall blond android in a spotless pale yellow suit appeared onstage.

Burdon scowled. "Which Shakespearean play is this supposed to be?"

"Beg pardon, sir. This is a projection of the visitor waiting downstairs in the foyer."

"Oh, yeah. The andy who works with Dr. Stolzer," he realized. "Send him up. And turn off the plays."

The stage went dark and a moment later the blond android entered the living room. "Good evening, Mr. Burdon," he said. "Dr. Stolzer is delayed, but he sent me in his place. My name is Deryk. That's D-e-r-y-k."

"Take a seat, Deryk," he invited. "I want to discuss the modifications to my dear sister's brain. There are a great many things the poor woman is going to have to forget."

"HOW DOES THIS LOOK, DARLIN'?" Marney emerged from a storeroom wearing a fluffy brunette wig. "Would you know it was me under this rug?"

"It's not exactly a foolproof disguise, *chiquita*, but it does alter your appearance some." He was in the process of stowing the still unconscious Avram Moyech in a large neowood crate labeled RED HOT PEPPERS.

Their skyvan, with a landing pattern already punched out, was dropping down toward the town of Balazo, Mexico.

Marney said, "Maybe you ought to get rid of that cute little mustache of yours."

"Nope, I'll keep it." He fitted the lid on the crate and secured it.

Bright multicolored lights were showing below in the night. Brassy music came flying up at them.

Returning to the pilot seat, Gomez said, "We've just about arrived. There's the Cantina Mall right over there."

There were several dozen cantinas and saloons in the five-acre, three-level mall. Their litesigns flashed colored names—*El Bufon, Café Tero, Ritmo Club, Trabajador, Mama Grande, Club Revancha, Cafe Granja.*

Gomez took over the controls just before their skyvan set down. He guided it to a landing on the far side of the landing area. They were only a few feet from the loading door of the El Bufon cantina.

Dropping free of the van, Gomez trotted over to the door. He whistled with his tongue against his teeth as he tapped three times.

"*¡Por Dios!*" exclaimed the slim, dark man who appeared in the doorway after the door slid open. "It's none other than Gomez!"

"I already phoned to alert you that I was coming, Raoul."

"I know, *sí,*" said Raoul Martinez. "But it's been a long time since I've seen you. I'm pleased and excited—and, after all, you're my second cousin."

"Third." Gomez held up three fingers.

"I feel closer than that. Ah . . . who's the *mujer?*"

Marney was walking toward them. "Is this the cousin who's goin' to help us?"

"Marney, meet Raoul."

Martinez shook her hand enthusiastically. "You have beautiful hair, *señorita.*"

"Why, thank you, Raoul. I owe it all to healthy livin' and a sensible diet."

Gomez coughed and pointed at the skyvan with his thumb. "The material I want shipped to Greater LA, *primo,* is in the van."

"I'll get a couple bots to unload it." Raoul grinned and headed back inside the cantina.

Clowns cavorted on the walls of the small office. The animated mural surrounded Gomez as he sat at the desk using the vidphone.

Marney was sitting demurely, knees together, on a rattan chair across the room.

From the phonescreen, frowning some, Bascom asked, "What kind of low bistro are you holed up in?"

"It's a cantina, *jefe*. Don't let the clown motif distract you," Gomez told him. "Simply attend to what I am telling you."

"Go ahead. But why the hell are clowns crawling all over the damned wall?"

"My esteemed cousin's cantina is named El Bufon. So he feels obliged to use buffoons and clowns in the decor," explained Gomez. "I'm shipping Avram Moyech to you by way of a very reliable, capable, and sneaky smuggling service my cousin happens to be affiliated with."

"Moyech is alive?"

"Ciertamente," he answered. "I just re-stunned the *pendejo* and he'll slumber in a babelike condition until he arrives at your doorstep. Where do you want him delivered?"

Bascom said, "At the agency in Greater LA. I'll pop down from Frisco to welcome him."

"He'll be there in approximately six or seven hours, *patrón,*" Gomez told him. "I only questioned the guy briefly, but he is definitely the one who rigged the tapes that make you look like a murderer."

Bascom smiled. "I'll see that Moyech gets turned over to Lieutenant Drexler in pristine shape—and in a talkative mood."

"Ahum," remarked Marney, giving Gomez a small wave.

"I'm in need, *jefe,* of a safe place to hide a friend of mine."

"Lady friend, is it?"

Marney came around to stand behind Gomez. Bending, she

smiled at the phone. "It's me, Mr. Bascom honey," she said, waving.

"Marney, are you still a gunslinger?"

"Well, more or less," she said. "Though sometimes I've had to take off my clothes. You'd be surprised how many folks aren't satisfied with just trick shootin'."

Bascom said, "I've got a couple of connections in that part of Mexico, Sid. I'll contact them and get back to you in under an hour."

"*Bueno,*" he said. "What sort of progress is Jake making?"

The chief of the Cosmos Detective Agency shook his head. "Something's come up."

"Is Jake okay?"

"He is, but Dan's been grabbed."

"By who—and where is he?"

"It ties in with my problems somehow," he said. "Jake thinks Dan's at the Junior Workers of America camp in McClennan, Mississippi."

"*¡Mierda!* Those places aren't exactly spas."

"Jake ought to be in the neighborhood by now. I set up a meeting between him and a tricky barrister named Gregory Krishovnik." Bascom rubbed a knuckle along the side of his nose. "He's a gent who ought to be able to help Jake extract his son from that place."

"By means other than legal?"

"That's Krishovnik."

Gomez said, "I'll stick here and see that Marney gets safely tucked away. Then I'm going to join Jake." He stood up. "Tell him to expect me."

36•T_{HE}

circular room was two floors high. The smooth neowood walls were tinted a pale underwater green. The only furnishings were a pair of black metal slingchairs.

Jake was seated in one. "Krishovnik claims you're an expert at this sort of operation, Menken," he was saying to the middle-sized, dark-haired man who occupied the facing chair.

"We've done a couple of very successful raids on Junior Workers of America camps hither and yon," answered Hershel Menken.

"I want to get my son out of Camp 30. Can you—"

"My organization—Menken's Marauders—can get anybody out

of anywhere, Cardigan," he said, standing. "Let me show you the planning room."

Jake rose and followed. "How many people do you use on an operation like this?"

"Never more than five."

"It'll be six this time—since I'm going along."

Menken opened a door by pressing his hand to the ID plate. "You're qualified," he said, crossing the threshold. "I researched you."

The large oval room was two floors high and filled with an assortment of electronics gear, including scanners, compscreens, holostages, and simulation tables.

Jake asked, "Can you tap the files of the camp? I want to be absolutely sure this Henry Weiner is actually my son Dan."

"Already did that—soon as Krishovnik contacted me." Menken pointed at the wall. "Screen 6 on your left."

Dan's image appeared on one of the many compscreens built into the wall.

Jake crossed to the eye-level screen. "Yeah, that's Dan. 'Weiner, Henry. Age—16.3 Home: Bristol, RI. Crime: grand theft, skycar. Sentence: five years.'"

"That's much too long to spend at Camp 30."

"We're going to have an extra problem rescuing him," said Jake, moving away from the image of his son. "It's pretty certain he's been mindwiped. So he's not going to recognize me when I show up to take him away."

"But *we'll* recognize him, Cardigan. We make our move, grab him, and depart." He walked to one of the simtables. "Let me show you what Camp 30 looks like."

Menken touched the controls and a miniature holographic image of the Junior Workers of America Camp 30 buildings, roads, and grounds materialized. Initially it was a bit fuzzy. After Menken whapped the side of the table with the heel of his hand the image became sharper and clearer.

"Twelve dorms," observed Jake. "Then three administration buildings. One main road and a few side roads."

"Over here at the edge of the woodlands," said Menken, pointing, "you'll notice three landvan garages. They're going to be important to our plan."

"More important than the guard towers at each corner of the setup?"

"The boys who are serving time at the camp spend their days doing manual labor," explained the leader of Menken's Marauders. "Road work, construction, farming, and similar occupations. All stuff that bots can do faster and more efficiently. But the camps look upon hard work as the chief punishment they have to administer."

"So every day the kids are taken out of 30 and delivered to the work sites?"

"Exactly, Cardigan." Menken turned off the table. "I'll gather my crew and we'll work out the details of a specific plan to extract your son from the Junior Workers."

"How long?"

Menken said, "I'd estimate we'll be ready to go no later than the day after tomorrow."

WHEN KACEY BASCOM stepped off the tennis court, after winning a match with the San Peligro Country Club probot, a large green robot was waiting for her on the simulated mosaic passway.

"Afternoon, mum." The mechanical man touched a green finger to his green forehead.

Halting, Kacey said, "Yes?"

"You'd be the associate of this Jake Cardigan bloke, wouldn't you?"

"Whom do you represent?"

"The gov wants to have a bit of a chat with you," explained the bot. "He was intending to share—make that sell—some tidbits of info to Cardigan. But, Lord, Cardigan ain't to be found on the whole blooming island."

"You must work for Monte Folkestone."

"That's dead right, mum," answered the robot. "If you was to stroll down to the beach and stop at the first immense, fat chap you see—that'd be the gov."

MONTE FOLKESTONE, wearing an ample flowered beach robe and a wide-brimmed sinstraw hat, was relaxing in a large and sturdy slingchair. He was sipping a chilled plazflask of Upper Kola and gazing through dark-tinted glasses out at the hazy afternoon sea. "Miss Bascom, so good to see you, my dear," he said as she approached him across the hot sand. "I take it your esteemed father is in good spirits in spite of his sorry plight?"

"You have something to sell?" She crouched beside his chair.

"Ah, right to business, is it? Admirable."

"Jake Cardigan is away—so you can deal directly with me."

"Such was my assumption, dear lady." The fat man chuckled. "If I'm not mistaken, you and the stalwart Mr. Cardigan are interested in the goings-on at yon NewTown plant."

"We are, yes."

Folkestone took another sip. "I've picked up some interesting items about Rebecca Burdon—her present situation and her probable future. Six hundred dollars."

"Cosmos will pay your fee. Tell me."

"Miss Burdon is presently the unwilling guest of her brother," said the fat man. "She's being detained in a separate wing of the facility." From a pocket of his flowery robe he took a folded sheet of fax paper and handed it to her. "This, dear child, will show you the exact location of her place of incarceration."

Taking it, Kacey said, "Why is Rowland Burdon doing this?"

"The unfortunate Rebecca has lately developed a conscience, it seems," he said, sighing. "That does tend to happen to some of us as we grow older. As I understand it, she threatened to expose her brother's evil deeds—which include manufacturing illegal Tek, murdering assorted enemies, being in cahoots with a Tek cartel, *and* participating in the framing of your dear papa."

"And Rebecca Burdon was planning to tell everything to the law?"

"She was, but, of course, that won't happen now."

"Why? Rowland can't keep her locked away in that place forever."

"By the end of the week it won't matter," explained Folkestone. "Rowland has brought in a nefarious sawbones named Dr. Stolzer. He's going to work on Rebecca's mind, cleansing it of all memories of Rowland's crimes, instilling a more positive outlook and pretty much turning her into a docile vegetable who'll make no further trouble for anyone."

"I'll have to get her out of there before they do that." Kacey stood up.

"If you need help in slipping into the NewTown—"

"No, thanks. I can take care of that myself." She left the fat man sitting there in the hot sun.

37 • WHEN

Jake came in through the back door of the boarded-up restaurant, Menken eased up out of the seat at the swayback counter and said, "Welcome to the Vegetable Bin, Cardigan."

There were two other people in the defunct dining room. A small, thin red-haired woman dressed in a gray slaxsuit and jacket was leaning against the wall that held dozens of rows of food-serving windows. Over by a lineup of vegetable juice machines, a lean, bearded man in his forties was tinkering with a juicer shaped like a huge carrot.

Jake inquired, "Why this place for a meeting?"

"Friend of mine still owns it and it makes a nice, quiet location for occasional meetings," answered the leader of Menken's

Marauders. "With an organization like ours, I don't like to have all our get-togethers at the same place—and this dump has, as you noticed coming in, a very effective security system still in place."

"Looks like they left you out in the sun too long, Jake," commented the thin woman. "You can't possibly be as old as all those wrinkles make you look. Of course, being just thirty myself, older people tend to appear—"

"Forty," said the tinkerer.

"Thirty-seven actually," she corrected, scowling.

Menken nodded Jake toward a seat in one of the booths and then slid in opposite him. "The young lady is Shawna Beck, driver/pilot and in charge of our transportation fleet. The fellow with the compulsion to repair things is Jess Kipling."

Kipling glanced up for a few seconds. "Howdy, Jake."

"He's our gadget man," explained Menken. "Looks after all our weapons, electronic equipment—and he cooks up anything special we need for our operations and raids."

Jake rested an elbow on the tabletop. "You're intending to try to rescue my son tomorrow morning?"

"We're *going* to rescue him," Menken informed him. "Dan, alias Henry Weiner, and seven other inmates of the JWA camp will leave their dorm at 8:03 A.M. tomorrow and be transported to a work site seven miles from 30."

"What is it?"

"They're building a side road on the outskirts of town. See, these kid camps believe that rough physical labor is a sure cure for antisocial behavior," said Menken.

Nodding, Jake asked, "You've got a map of their route tomorrow morning?"

"We'll have it as soon as Van Horn, our topography expert, arrives. Then we'll go over everybody's part in the operation."

"You sure you're up to a strenuous job like this, Jake?" Shawna had moved over to lean against the wall beside their booth.

"Menken's Marauders," he reminded her, "are noted for their easygoing camaraderie and admirable team spirit. Quit nagging Cardigan, sweet."

"A simple tactical question, Hersh," responded the thin woman. "Usually our easygoing team doesn't include strangers."

Jake grinned. "We're expecting another stranger shortly—so brace yourself, Shawna."

"Jesus! Not another old fogey?"

"Sid Gomez is a mere youth compared to me," he assured her. "He's my partner at the Cosmos Detective Agency out in—"

"Cosmos Half-assed Bureaucracy," was her opinion. "Big bunch of bumbling, arrogant gumshoes charging ridiculous fees for simple little piddly investigating chores."

Jake nodded. "That's our motto, yeah."

Menken made an impatient shooing gesture with his right hand. "Wander off and meditate for a while, Shawna," he advised. "It's a policy of the house not to insult the paying customers."

She gave a lopsided shrug and headed for another part of the restaurant. "Maybe the bylaws ought to be amended."

From the room that had once been the pantry of the Vegetable Bin came the sound of people arriving.

Menken's hand moved closer to his shoulder holster.

Jake turned to look toward that doorway. Then he relaxed and grinned. "I was just discussing your many merits, Sid," he said.

Gomez, looking somewhat weary and worn, was being escorted by a large, pudgy black man. *"Buenas noches,"* he said, his voice sounding a little worn.

"Holy Christ," commented Shawna, "this one's in even worse shape than Jake."

"Who's the cordial *mujer?*" inquired the detective as he joined his partner in the booth, sliding in next to Menken.

Jake said, "Each member of Menken's Marauders has a specialty. Shawna Beck is the hospitality chairman."

"She's very good at it."

Shawna produced a rude noise. "A wiseass on top of all his other obvious flaws."

Smiling in her direction, Gomez said, "Fortunately, *cara*, I became a stoic just yesterday. Now rude remarks roll off my back and I no longer deliver a brisk kick in the slats to anyone who makes one."

"Enough of this." Menken offered his hand to Gomez. "I'm Hershel Menken and I run, as you can probably guess from the name, Menken's Marauders."

Jake said, "Sid, we're going to spring Dan tomorrow morning."

"*Mañana*, huh? You're sure, then, it is Dan, *amigo?*"

"There's no doubt. They rechristened him Henry Weiner and faked his background, but it's Dan."

Looking up at the dusty ceiling, Gomez remarked, "We've worked with a wide variety of tipsters and informants over the years, but this is just about the first psychic."

"Susan Grossman was right about all this," said Jake. "So I'm, though sort of skeptical, a convert."

"It isn't possible, do you think, Jake, that she came upon this information in some less magical manner?"

"How?"

"Oh, her dead old dad might be in cahoots with a Teklord or with somebody high up in NewTown Pharmaceuticals," he suggested. "She could simply have overheard something and is trying to pass it off as a supernatural message."

"Nope. From what Molly Fine tells me, this is legit."

Menken glanced from Jake to Gomez. "I have great faith in extrasensory powers," he said. "I'm extremely open-minded."

"Empty-headed," muttered Shawna, who was watching the lanky Kipling putter with the giant carrot.

38 • BAScom

blanked the windows of his tower office and the twilight city vanished. "Why the hangdog expression, Anselmo?" he asked from behind his desk.

Roy Anselmo was sitting in a plastiglass chair facing his boss. He ran a hand through his feathery blond hair, contemplated his feet, glanced at the blank viewindows. "We've never exactly, Walt, seen eye to eye on the methods of either Jake Cardigan or Sid Gomez," he said.

"The truth shouldn't make you uneasy."

Anselmo looked directly at the agency chief. "Jake shouldn't have been allowed to abandon work on your case."

"He took some time off. He didn't desert the sinking ship."

"Your life is on the line, Walt. It's unforgivable for him to—"

"So is his son's." Bascom made an impatient dismissive gesture with his right hand. "I don't have a problem with the way Jake's handling things. So there's no need for you to."

Anselmo cleared his throat. "Then there's Gomez," he said. "What he did in regard to Avram Moyech just isn't right."

"He tracked down the bozo who helped frame me, Roy," reminded Bascom. "Moyech will be arriving here fairly soon now. Fact is, I just got confirming word that delivery will be made shortly."

"From my reading of Gomez's report on this matter—which is as terse and cocky as all of his reports—he kidnapped the man."

"He made, rather, a citizen's arrest."

"*And* he entered into a conspiracy with smugglers to get Moyech to the agency."

"I'm figuring that the guy's testimony will help clear me. Seems to me, Roy, that you ought to be glad about that."

"Moyech's testimony is one thing, Walt," said the detective, "but I have a fear that the methods Gomez is using will taint everything."

"Naw, it won't hurt—not after I smooth the rough edges. Now, do you have—"

"Police officer here to see you, sir," broke in the desk vidphone.

"Who?"

"Lieutenant Drexler of the SoCal force."

Bascom drummed the fingers of his right hand in sequence on his desktop. He sighed and instructed, "Send the guy in."

The black policeman entered, walking fast and looking grim. "Evening, Walt. Roy."

"Another sourpuss," commented Bascom.

"How's that?"

"Merely the ramblings of a doddering old coot. Why are you here, Lieutenant?"

Drexler stopped next to Anselmo's chair and looked down at Bascom. "Aren't you in enough trouble already, Walt?"

"Are you here to offer me more?"

The policeman said, "I'm here to investigate a report that you're involved with kidnapping and smuggling."

ON THE HOLOSTAGE, a life-size J. J. Bracken bounced twice in his high-back black metal chair and jabbed a finger in the direction of the uniformed guest in the facing chair. "Tell us about this thousand-dollar-a-week Tek habit of yours, Colonel Woodbine," he invited, brushing back an unruly lock of his pale blond hair.

"I don't have a thousand-dollar-a-week Tek habit," insisted the colonel, a heavyset man in the tan uniform of the National Army.

"More than a thousand dollars, then?"

"I'm not addicted to Tek, you offensive scoundrel. I agreed to appear on your disgusting *Facin' Bracken* broadcast to answer your recent slanderous attacks on the American Cyborg Rights Organization. Not to have my reputation muddied over."

"So it's not true, then, not true, that you are a hopeless Tekkie? Not true despite the huge amount of data I have access to, that you have long been tapping the fat treasury of your subversive organization to pay your mounting bills for illegal electronic stimulants?"

"I won't remain here if you—"

"And it's not true, not true, that you're also involved in a sneaky plan to manufacture Tek in a clandestine setup with a legitimate—"

"Darn," said Kacey Bascom, who was sitting in one of the two occupied chairs in the entertainment room of the seaside villa. "He's going to spill the news before I can even get inside NewTown."

"How's that, Kacey?" inquired the pinkish man sitting next to her.

"Nothing, Mr. Temmerson."

On the stage the colonel was hopping up out of his chair. He lunged, swinging at the host with his coppery cyborg right fist. "This ends the interview, sir," he explained as he punched Bracken twice in the jaw and sent him stumbling back to fall completely out of the picture.

Without taking his eyes off the stage, Temmerson asked, "What were you saying, young lady?"

"Oh, nothing."

Colonel Woodbine strode angrily off the stage. Seconds later two large white robots lifted J. J. Bracken into view and arranged him in his high-back black chair.

"You can see, see clearly, how people like Colonel Woodbine work," he told his audience. Then he rubbed at his jaw. "He and his organization, swilling at the public trough, are bully boys. Violence, and not pure sweet reason, is their tool; violence and lying; violence, lying, and disloyalty to just about every basic American virtue and value, every value and virtue." He slumped slightly. "Well, that's all the time we have for now. On my next eagerly awaited *Facin' Bracken* I'll have the notorious Emily Briarcliff facing me and trying, in her annoyingly mild-mannered way, to explain the incredible boondoggles that have been uncovered at the SoCal Home for Orphans. I'll also be telling you how to order, how to get one for your very own, my new vidisk *Throw All the Freeloading Orphans into the Gutter Where They Belong.*"

Temmerson turned off the stage with the control in his seat arm. "The man's inspirational."

"Yes, isn't he?" Kacey smiled. "I want to go into the NewTown setup tomorrow."

"That can be arranged. Which delivery shift?"

"Morning, if possible."

"Your associate will be accompanying you. Mr. Carrington, was it?"

"Cardigan. No, he's away for a few days."

"You're going to do this alone?"

"There's a time factor here, Mr. Temmerson. I have to."

"Very brave. But you'd have to be working for a man like J. J. Bracken." He lowered his voice. "Does this have something to do with what he was hinting about Tek on tonight's show?"

"You've guessed it. But, please, don't mention this to anyone."

"I have too much respect for J. J. Bracken and you to do anything like that, young lady."

"What time should I report to your Foodz plant?"

"No later than eight A.M. Shall I send a skylimo for you?"

"I'll get there on my own, thanks."

"It's a great thrill to be helping someone I admire as much as J. J. Bracken."

"I can imagine," said Kacey.

39•A

light mist had come drifting in across the Pacific with the night, and the Malibu Sector of Greater Los Angeles had a hazy, blurred look. The brightlit towers, the interlacing, multilevel pedramps and walkways, the skycars and skycabs floating by all appeared smudged. There was a strong scent of the sea in the air. Even in the plastiglass tracking shed in the landing area atop the Cosmos tower you could smell it.

"They should be setting down in about six minutes," Bascom was saying.

Lieutenant Drexler looked from the screen, which showed an image of a yellow skyvan marked BORDERLAND PRODUCTS, LTD.

descending down through the misty night, up into the misty sky itself. "I'm still," he said, holding his thumb and forefinger several inches apart, "at least that far from being convinced, Walt."

"You know all about Avram Moyech and his career, Lieutenant. You've even arrested the gent several times."

"I admit Moyech is a very talented vid forger." He was still looking skyward through the plastiglass roof. "But you haven't convinced me he's good enough to produce security tapes that'd fool our experts."

"Yet he did that very thing."

"You say."

"True. But, better yet, *he* says."

"Not to you. Not to me so far."

"He confided in Gomez."

The black cop laughed. "Gomez is not my idea of a reliable source of the truth."

"Funny, he always lists you among his favorite people on the face of the Earth."

"I'll question Moyech," said Lieutenant Drexler. "And make sure he answers."

"This is a complex business that's going on."

"You mean there's more to it than your going goofy with jealousy and knocking off your rival?"

"C'mon, Lieutenant. I can outcharm any rival I ever ran into. I don't have to shoot the competition," Bascom assured him. "Moyech was linked to the Zack Excoffon Tek cartel up in NorCal. There's a plot afoot to set up a huge Tek manufacturing plant down in the Caribbean with a cover of—"

"Señor Bascom, Señor Bascom!" A voice suddenly came booming out of the voxbox.

The Cosmos chief activated the talkback. "Yeah, what?"

"This is Raoul Martinez," said the voice. "We're nearly to your headquarters."

"Good, but is something wrong?"

"*¡Sí, muy malo!* We've lost our power and—*¡Dios!*"

"There they are." Drexler was in the open doorway of the shed, pointing up into the misty night.

The yellow skyvan was dropping down too rapidly, and in a wild zigzag way.

"Martinez!" cried Bascom.

". . . out of control . . ."

The nose of the plummeting van sideswiped the side of a high pedramp. Light globes started smashing all along the guardrail, the rails were snapping, a series of long jagged cracks went snaking along the ramp. Pedestrians were tripping and falling, shouting, crying out.

The skyvan hit another ramp. A heavyset woman screamed, fell through a broken railing. More big globes of yellow light popped, a huge glosign advertising NewTown's Upmood was ripped free of its moorings and went spinning and smashing down toward the distant ground.

Drexler yanked out his handphone. "Malibu Sector—Cosmos vicinity!" he yelled. "Skyvan crash, civilian injuries, fires, considerable damage! Get on it!"

The skyvan, with Avram Moyech inside, smashed into yet another pedramp. It remained there, and then came an immense roaring explosion.

The craft came apart like a huge jigsaw puzzle, and its parts and its people were scattered violently across the blurred night. A jagged chunk that had BORDERLAND on it spun away and smashed into the display window of a skytravel agency; PRODUCTS hit a passing skycab smack in the engine, and there was another explosion.

Dark smoke came billowing out of the skyvan to mix with the fog, and everything turned a sad, sooty gray.

Drexler said quietly, "There goes your witness, Walt."

THE FOG WAS THICK in the Santa Barbara Sector of Greater LA. Susan Grossman was sitting out on the deck of the beach house where she was a guest. The one-way plastiglass dome kept out the night chill—kept anyone from seeing her—yet allowed the young woman to watch the dark, foggy ocean. "This is very pleasant," she was saying to Molly Fine. "Thank your Uncle Leo for me."

"His friends are up vacationing on the Moon and they owe him a favor. So you have this place to hide out in," Molly told her friend. "Uncle Leo mentioned to me that he hoped you wouldn't have any gun battles here."

"I'll make a serious effort, but I don't have much control over that." Her smile was faint and brief.

"How've you been doing?"

"Well, I'm not especially joyful. But it has been pleasant living this way—with just servos and robots," she answered. "Androids and people take a lot more effort."

"Most often, yes. And they're much harder to order around."

Susan twisted her fingers together. "Typical of me, complaining of my problems. What about Dan?"

"As I told you, he is where you said."

"Yes, I know. I'm never wrong about things like that," she said. "I'm not bragging, I just mean the visions are never wrong—not so far, anyway."

"Well, Jake Cardigan is in Mississippi, too."

"What's he going to do?"

"Get Dan out."

"You mean he'll go to the authorities and—"

"Nope, I don't think he intends to be especially law-abiding about this."

"A prison break—something like that?"

Smiling, Molly shook her head. "Jake didn't give me any details about what, how, or when. But I got the impression he expects to have Dan out of that rotten camp soon," she answered. "This way, though, I can't give anything away, since I don't know the details."

After a silent moment, Susan said, "I had another one."

Molly left her chair, crossing to her friend. "About Dan? Tell me what you saw."

"No, not about Dan." Susan touched Molly's arm. "I'm sorry if I got your hopes up. No, this was a very brief one and had to do with Rebecca Burdon."

"She's co-owner of NewTown Pharmaceuticals—and they're deeply mixed up in this whole mess."

"Rebecca's a friend of my father. I met her a few times at parties the twins gave," she went on. "I've never—so far, anyway—had a vision about someone I didn't know."

Molly knelt next to the chair. "What exactly did you see?"

Susan frowned. "It was strange, really. Rebecca's down on San Peligro, that island in the Caribbean," she said. "But they've got her locked away in a suite inside the NewTown facility. What I saw—well, she was trying to get out, shouting, pounding on the door of her living room. Sort of like me at Dr. Stolzer's. Two bots came in, grabbed Rebecca, and gave her some kind of injection. They were very rough with her, and after she passed out they dragged her into the bedroom and tossed her on the bed. Her head was hanging over the side and her clothes were all messed up. The whole damn suite, by the way, is very well furnished. It's no prison cell, but Rebecca Burdon is sure as hell a prisoner."

"I'd better let somebody at Cosmos know about this—in case they don't already," said Molly thoughtfully. "Would her twin brother let them treat her like that?"

Susan said, "Rowland Burdon's a real shit, Molly. If she disappears for good and all, I wouldn't be surprised."

Molly said, rising up, "My Uncle Anthony says to tell you he's just about got a hearing for you arranged. It'll only take a few more days and he's certain he can get you declared competent and independent. Your father will no longer be able to commit you anyplace, and you can live by yourself. You'll be free."

"Free," Susan said softly. "I wonder if I can manage that."

40●I N

his dream Hank was someplace distant from Camp 30. It was warm there and the morning sun was bright. He was walking along the beach, feeling good, and a man was coming toward him, grinning, waving. He almost remembered the man's name, but then it slipped away. The man called out something to him, but Hank couldn't catch what he said.

Then an intense pain started in his hip and went racing down his left leg. The leg jerked, he cried out, and sat up wide awake.

"Off your ox, Weiner!"

Two gunmetal robots loomed over his gray cot. The one was slapping the shockstik he'd just used on Hank in the metallic palm of his hand. Stenciled across his broad chest in white was GUARD 11A.

The other bot was GUARD 14B.

14B said, "Get up, Hank. Get your ass dressed."

Rubbing his eyes, Hank stood. His left leg gave out on him and he stumbled. He bumped into 11A and held on to maintain his balance.

"None of that." 11A prodded him with the shockstik again.

Hank doubled up, swayed, and then fell back onto the cot.

Ogden Whitney awakened on the next cot. He got up and pulled Hank to his feet. "What are you guys doing to him?"

"Stay out of this, Ogden," warned 14B.

"Hank's got a new assignment," explained 11A as he gave the black youth a prod with the shockstik.

Ogden grimaced, fisted his hands, and dropped to his knees.

"I'm supposed to be on the roadwork gang," said Hank, his voice dry and rusty sounding.

"Not anymore, kid," 14B told him. "Come on, get your clothes on. The landvan is here to take you to the sewer project."

A SHARP MORNING WIND was blowing through the forest area along the rutted Mississippi back road. Across the way in a small roadside clearing stood a ramshackle little neowood-and-plastiglass restaurant. Its weathered litesign proclaimed it THE BREAKFAST NOOK, and through its dusty windows you could see a half dozen or so customers scattered at its small tables. Parked in front of the place were a dented skycar, a rickety old landtruck, and two aging electrocars.

Menken, crouched beside Jake in the brush, was using his hand voxphone to talk to Shawna, who was in the landtruck with Kipling. "Okay, the camp landvan should be rolling by at about

8:17," he was saying. "Is everybody in place on your side of the road?"

"Sure, I just checked them."

"After Kip uses the disabler on the van, Jake and I will move out and take care of the driver and the guard. Gomez and Petway will disable the follow-up car and incapacitate the two camp guards riding in that."

"How's the old gent making out?" she inquired.

Grinning, Jake borrowed the phone. "Glad you asked," he said. "Will you have time to pop across the road and help me get to my feet just as the action starts? My back's been acting up and—"

"You're not even as funny as that long-winded Latino pal of yours." She ended the call.

"Don't mind Shawna," advised Menken as he retrieved the phone. "She's often nastiest to the people she likes the best."

"Then I must be the love of her life."

The day was gradually brightening and the wind felt a bit warmer now.

Glancing at Jake, the leader of the Marauders said, "We do this sort of thing very well."

"So I've heard," said Jake. "If this involved simply a Cosmos client, I wouldn't be uneasy. When it's my son—"

"Hold it—call coming in." The phone had commenced vibrating faintly in his hand. "Yeah?"

A voice unfamiliar to Jake said, "A snag."

"Explain."

"Boy won't be on the truck."

"Shit, where is he?" asked Menken.

"Reassigned to Work Crew 7. Sewer project."

"Has that landvan left 30 yet?"

"Six minutes ago. You owe me another $250."

Menken let the phone drop to his side for a few seconds. Then he made a call. "Shawna, we've got to get over to Route 57 quick. Dan Cardigan is in the camp van heading for the old Marsh Plantation."

"What went wrong?"

"Nothing, except they put him in a new work gang. Move." He was up and running to where they'd hidden their skycar.

"Can you guys bring this off?" Jake was close behind him.

"I think we sure as hell better try, don't you?"

"Yep."

41•REBECCA

Burdon didn't bother to turn toward the door when it opened behind her. She remained sitting, arms folded, in the hard white armchair, absently looking at the endlessly repeating beach view on the wallscreen. The same five gulls had drifted across the screen ninety-four times since she'd seated herself.

"Have your medical toadies arrived, Rollo?"

A hand tapped her gently on the shoulder.

Looking up, Rebecca saw a young woman standing there dressed in dark slax and a white medical tunic. Frowning, she said, "Aren't you—"

Kacey made a "don't talk" gesture. Then she hurried over to the nearest wall, slipped a bug-disabler disk out of her pocket, and stuck it against a panel. "That'll give us a few unobserved minutes," she said. "Yes, I'm Kacey Bascom."

"Do you know what my brother's trying to do to your father?"

"Got a pretty good notion, yes," she answered. "Are you willing to talk to the SoCal cops about what you know?"

"I'll talk to anybody who'll listen." She stood up. "I can't abide what's going on."

"I can get you clear of here. But we have to go right now."

"I've no reason to linger, Kacey."

"I came in on a Foodz skyvan. We can, with luck, get out that way, too."

"And why the medical outfit?"

"Oh, I acquired a fake ID packet that implies I'm an assistant to Dr. Stolzer."

"That bastard," observed Rebecca. "My brother's hired him to arrange some memory loss for me."

"He hasn't started working on you yet?"

"Not yet, but soon." She moved to the door. "Would we have time—and can you get us there—to visit the Tek wing?"

"We've got exactly seventeen minutes. Why?"

"There might be a way to throw a spanner into Rowland's whole clandestine Tek operation here," she answered. "When the plant was built, down in the bowels of this place, they included a destruction switch. In the case of a raid, you know. I know where it is and how to activate it."

Kacey smiled. "That would make a nice farewell gesture, wouldn't it?" She reached toward the door.

But the door came sliding open before she touched it.

A large, wide man, dark and wearing a loose gray suit, entered the room. "I understand you work for Dr. Stolzer, young lady."

"I do and Miss Burdon is one of our patients."

The large man took another step toward Kacey, still smiling.

"Odd that I don't have any idea who you are," he told her. "Especially since I'm Dr. Stolzer."

HANK WAS SITTING on the bench that ran along the left side of the Camp 30 landvan. He shared it with three other young men, and there were four more JWA boys in the other side of the chugging, rattling landvan.

"What'd you do now?" asked the pale blond youth next to him.

"Hum?"

"To get yourself put on this shit detail."

Hank shrugged. "Don't know. I tell you, Burt, I'm not even sure why I'm at Camp 30 at all."

"Yeah, Ogden told me. They mindwiped you, more than likely," said Burt as he scratched his side and looked out at the dusty road and the woodlands they were rolling through. "They do that with the tough cases."

"Think that's what I am?"

"Figure it out, Hank. You must be or they wouldn't treat you like this."

"Guess that's right."

"You've been switched to the worst work detail you can get," continued Burt. "And they used a shockstik on you this morning. They don't do that with everybody."

Hank said, "You know, I've been having dreams. About someplace else—not Mississippi or Rhode Island, where they say I come from."

Laughing, the blond boy said, "Hell, everybody dreams about a better place than Camp 30."

"No, but I mean I—"

"What the hell!" exclaimed the cyborg driver and hit the brakes.

As the landvan came to a lurching, rattling halt, the robot guard who was sitting next to the driver started to swing up the arm that had a lazgun built into it.

A skycar had come swooping down out of the morning sky and landed directly in the path of the van.

"Another one!" Burt was pointing at the back window.

Another skycar was setting down back there, directly in the path of the backup car.

And a third skycar was skimming in across the weedy field on their right.

"Trouble?" asked Hank.

"For these bastards, sure," said Burt, laughing. "But maybe not for us."

MENKEN SET DOWN the skycar at the edge of the road. "Going fine so far," he observed while getting clear of his safety gear. "Kip and Shawna stopped the landvan and, looks like from here, took out the driver and the guardbot."

"Let's hope so." Jake went out of the car, stungun drawn, and ran to the backside of the halted Camp 30 landvan.

Up on the road, Gomez and the husky black Petway were using stunguns to take care of the three guards who'd come diving out of the backup car.

Sprinting, Jake grabbed the rear door of the van and yanked it open. He jumped inside, ducked low.

And there was Dan, sitting between a blond boy and a hefty Chinese youth. "Okay, fellas," announced Jake. "Everybody out."

"You springing us or is this a hijacking?" asked the blond boy.

"You're on your own. Get over to the crimson skyvan that's just landing and you'll get transported to safe ground."

Seven of them, laughing and shouting, went stumbling out into the morning.

But Dan remained seated.

Jake, grinning, approached him. "Dan, are you okay?"

He stared up at Jake. "My name—well, at least that's what they tell me—my name is Hank, sir."

"No, you're Dan Cardigan," Jake told him. "I'm your father."

He studied Jake's face. "That would be great, but . . ." He shook his head sadly. "I just don't remember you, sir."

"Then just trust me, Dan. We've got to get the hell out of here." He took his son's arm, guided him out onto the dusty road.

Gomez met them. *"Bueno,"* he reported. "We coldcocked all three of those *pendejos* back there. Hi, Daniel."

Dan asked, "Am I supposed to know you, too, sir?"

"Mindwiped," said Jake quietly.

"You used to," Gomez informed him. "I'm the incomparable Sid Gomez. Friend and partner of your dad and a first-class sleuth by trade."

"Biography later," said Jake impatiently. "Sid, Dan and I will share your skycar. Petway'll switch to Menken's. Let's go."

"Sí, a change of venue is definitely what's called for."

The three of them ran to Gomez's skycar.

As they were climbing in Dan said, "Thanks for helping me, sir."

42●

I_T was midday and the two skycars were parked near each other in a small clearing of woods in a Mississippi town that was neither Yazoo nor McClennan.

Menken said, "Everything went damn well, Cardigan."

"Yeah, your Marauders were great. Even Shawna."

The thin woman was leaning against the door of one of the cars. "You hobbled around pretty well yourself," she conceded.

"What of me, *chiquita?*" inquired Gomez.

"You're nearly impossible, but at least you didn't foul us up too much."

Jake put his hand on his son's shoulder. "You understand what's going to happen now, Dan?"

"Yes, but I still don't believe I'm going to turn out to be anybody named Dan Cardigan, sir," he said. "Still it sounds like a better deal than being Hank Weiner."

"Involves you with fewer sewers," Gomez pointed out.

"Maggie Pennoyer is a friend of mine back in New England—in Connecticut," he explained to his son. "Her specialty is working with people who've been mindwiped or otherwise had their memories and identities futzed up."

"I understand, sir."

"Shawna and Menken are going to take you there, Dan," he said. "I've already set everything up with Maggie. She'll work with you and—probably in just a few days—you'll have your mind and your real self back."

"That would be terrific."

Jake said, "Sid and I have to go back down to San Peligro Island in the Caribbean to finish up the case we're working on. Soon as I'm through there, I'll join you at Maggie's hideaway."

Dan held out his hand and they shook. "Good-bye, sir."

Jake watched while his son got into the skycar with Menken and the woman. The craft came to life, then went climbing up into the early afternoon.

Jake sighed. "I wish," he said, "just once, he'd called me Dad."

KACEY BASCOM BLUSHED. She brought her hand up to her mouth. "Gosh, don't I feel silly," she said to Dr. Stolzer.

He pushed further into the room. "What precisely are you up to—and who the hell are you?"

She giggled, pressed her hand to her chest. "Oh, it's really a stupid sort of prank, Doctor," she said. "See, I bet my . . ."

Her hand snapped to her shoulder holster and she was holding a stungun. She pressed it into the big doctor's chest and fired.

Stolzer made a surprised huffing sound. His mouth snapped open as his eyes suddenly shut. Each of his hands inscribed invisible circles in the air. Then he did a few steps of a tiptoe dance and dropped to his knees.

Kacey shut the door and booted him in the back.

The doctor fell over flat out. "I hope he's the last unexpected item we have to face today."

Rebecca was staring at her. "You shot him very calmly, Kacey," she said with admiration.

"Something I learned in the days I was a cop," she said. "You still want to try to destroy the Tek lab?"

"I'd like to attempt it."

Kacey moved over beside the sprawled Dr. Stolzer. "Wish I had time to give this guy a mindwipe." She bent and dragged him across the room, leaving him behind the armchair. "We can leave now."

"It's too bad you and I have such different political views," remarked Rebecca. "Otherwise we could probably be close friends."

"We can talk politics later." Kacey opened the door, took a cautious glance out. "We can make our move now."

THE LAB WAS long and low and mostly white. Forty white-enameled robots were working at rows of tables and desks, manufacturing Tek chips. The air was faintly scented with lemon.

Rowland Burdon escorted the android Deryk into the facility. "I think you'll enjoy seeing this"—he stopped immediately inside the doorway—"since you're involved in working with the mind. It's the best and most efficient Tek laboratory outside of Europe."

"Very impressive," commented the andy.

"And our chips can be manufactured at a much lower cost than those of most of the Tek cartels."

Deryk moved further into the room, watching the nearest bots at their work. "Dr. Stolzer and I have found that most of the criticisms of Tek—the claim that it's so dangerously addictive and that it can cause seizures and brain damage—are considerably exaggerated," he told his host, smiling. "Dr. Stolzer has long been an active supporter of the campaign to legalize Tek."

"If Tek were legal, it would really screw up this part of our business." From his pocket Burdon took a small NewTown needlegun.

"What's that you're using?"

While he searched for a place on his lower arm to place the tip of the gun, Burdon replied, "New product we're testing. Delivers a dose of euphoria serum that's completely effective yet totally non-addictive."

"I notice, though, that this is the third time you've used it since we began our little tour of your plant," mentioned Deryk. "Could it be, if not addictive, at least highly habit forming?"

"No, perfectly safe," he said, dropping the gun back into his pocket. "I'm simply interested in giving it a very thorough test."

"Are you more euphoric now than you were an hour ago?"

"Most certainly, of course. In fact, I feel—"

A faint tremor had begun underfoot. The lab floor had started vibrating.

"What's wrong?" Deryk was scowling down at the floor.

Burdon tugged out a handphone. "Central Control," he demanded.

The floor increased its shaking and now the white walls of the lab were rattling.

The robots kept on working, even though the lab tables and the desks were shaking with increasing violence.

"Central Control, goddamn it!" shouted Burdon into his phone.

"Hadn't we better get out of here?" suggested the android.

"Not until I find out what the hell is going on."

Instead of a voice, a harsh squealing sound was coming out of the earpiece.

Rumbling explosions began on the other side of one of the walls. Then a huge hole was blown in the wall and a gust of roaring flame came shooting in. It ate across tables and robots, burning up everything, turning everything black and crusty.

"Jesus!" cried Burdon. "Somebody's activated the destruct system."

He turned and tried to run.

43•MAYBE,

possibly," said Lieutenant Drexler, "I was wrong about you, Walt—or partially wrong, anyway. It's just possible you're not a conniving murderer after all."

"I'm touched," Bascom informed him.

"Maybe."

They were in Lieutenant Drexler's large office at the SoCal Police Center in the Santa Monica Sector of Greater LA.

"My version of what happened to Dwight Grossman is starting to sound a shade more plausible, Lieutenant?"

The policeman gave a grudging nod. He was behind his desk, hand poised over a control panel. On the wall, one of the comp-screens showed a head shot of the late Avram Moyech. "I'm ready to agree that this guy had the ability to turn out forged tapes good enough to fool us," he said slowly. "And the information you got from that henchman of Zack Excoffon seems to make it clear that they did hire Moyech to do something for the Excoffon Tek cartel."

"Drexler, old pal, I also showed you copies of Moyech's Banx records—decoded ones that indicate he did get dough from them."

"Records don't say for what."

Bascom, who was perched on the edge of the policeman's desk, said, "The gent was blown to glory last night—just before arriving at Cosmos. That ain't just a coincidence."

"No, that's one of the things that makes your story convincing," admitted the lieutenant. "Even you aren't duplicitous enough, Walt, to blow up a van full of people to frame Excoffon."

"I'll come to you next time I need a character reference."

"But this other stuff you're trying to pass off on me," he said, shaking his head. "I mean, the Burdons are—"

"Yeah, upright citizens, pillars of society, a credit to the GLA community. Even so, Rowland is in cahoots with Excoffon to turn out Tek."

"Down in the Caribbean, huh?"

"So we believe. My daughter's down there right now looking into this—and Jake Cardigan'll be back with her today."

"If anybody's an expert on Tek, it's that bastard Cardigan. A user and a convicted dealer."

"C'mon, he was framed on that."

"I know the guy was Tekhead."

"For a while, long time ago. Not now, and he never worked for the cartels or sold as much as a single Tek chip."

"Your opinion."

A voxbox on his desk said, "Turn on the Newz Channel, Lieutenant Drexler."

"Christ, now what?" He touched the control panel.

". . . at least a third of the NewTown Pharmaceuticals plant here in this Caribbean paradise," a beautiful red-haired newscaster was saying.

Behind her, glaring in the sun, the NewTown facility could be seen with flames and smoke rising out of one side of it.

"According to a spokesman for NewTown, the exact cause of the accident is unknown at this time," she continued. "Most of the damage was apparently caused by a series of belowground explosions. The personnel in this seriously damaged wing was entirely robot and android, we are told. There are, at this moment, no confirmed reports of any human deaths."

Old footage of Rowland and Rebecca Burdon, enjoying themselves at a vast party, replaced the picture of the burning plant.

"Neither Rowland Burdon nor his twin sister, Rebecca, socialite owners of the vast NewTown Pharmaceuticals organization, are available for comment. Indeed, the current whereabouts of either of the Burdons are unknown."

"Going to be hard to prove the guy was bootlegging Tek," said Drexler. "I'm nurturing a hunch that what blew up down there was the Tek lab."

"I'd bet on that, too." Bascom stood up. "I'll leave you now, Lieutenant. I want to contact my daughter."

"Think she had something to do with the fireworks?"

"No, but once in a while I feel a fatherly concern for her."

JAKE WAS LEANING forward in the passenger seat of their skycar. "Damn, I can't contact Kacey Bascom anywhere," he said as he turned off the vidphone built into the dash.

"We'll be on the island in about fifty minutes, *amigo*," said Gomez. "Once there, we'll track her down."

"I'm wondering if she tried to go inside the NewTown plant alone."

"She's a capable *mujer*. Don't fret." He eyed his partner for a few seconds. "Are you developing an interest in her?"

"Avuncular maybe, not romantic."

The phone buzzed. "Yeah?" answered Jake, activating it again.

Walt Bascom appeared on the screen. "You lads nearing San Peligro?"

"Less than an hour away," answered Jake.

"Quite a few things have happened on that tropical paradise since you left town, Jake. Have you heard about the NewTown plant?"

"No. What happened?"

"They're not letting out any details, but it sounds to me like the whole damn secret Tek lab Burdon was running there went flooey and blew up."

"How the hell did that happen?"

Bascom smiled. "Well, in a way, my daughter had a hand in it."

"So she did go in there alone."

"She had to. She found out—from one of your informants, in fact—that Burdon had his sister locked up inside the place," the chief of the Cosmos Agency informed him. "He was planning to have our chum Dr. Stolzer do a mindwipe on her and thus keep her from telling anybody about his many shady activities."

"That son of a bitch Stolzer is probably the one who mindwiped Dan, too."

"That sort of thing is a specialty with him," said Bascom. "But look, you can get all the details from Kacey as to how she sprung Rebecca Burdon out of there and how Rebecca took care of the Tek lab. What I want you and Gomez to do is get her and the Burdon woman off the island and back here to Greater LA.

Rebecca is eager to tell Drexler and any other lawman who wants to listen all about how her dear sibling set me up."

Gomez inquired, "Where do we find them, *jefe?*"

"It's a place called the Villa Sombra, way up in the hills on the north side of the island," replied Bascom. "Contact of mine loaned it to them for me. I've got a half dozen local ops guarding it, but I need you two to help Kacey get this lady away safe."

"We'll do it," promised Jake.

Gomez said, "Did Rowland Burdon blow up with the lab?"

"Informed sources don't agree about that," said Bascom. "Some say he was inside the place when it blew and that he's now part of the debris. Other reports maintain he's still above the ground."

"We'll have to assume he's alive and watch out for him," said Jake.

"Any other news items we ought to have, *jefe?*"

"Well, the International Weather Service is predicting a hurricane for midnight tonight. So it might be a good idea to get the hell off the island before then." He left the screen.

"Muy bien," said Gomez, smiling. "This is turning into the sort of case I enjoy. We've got damsels in distress, rascally villains, and a possible chance to battle nature itself."

44•T<small>HE</small>

wind arrived earlier than anticipated. There was an intense clarity in the sky in the moments before sundown. The palms on the sharply slanting hillside outside the living room of the Villa Sombra began to rattle faintly, and gradually an odd sighing could be heard all around.

"The hurricane is definitely on the way," observed Rebecca Burdon, stopping beside one of the viewindows.

"I just talked to Jake on the vidphone," said Kacey, who was pacing the big living room. "He and his partner will be here in a few minutes. Then we'll get off the island."

Rebecca said, "Your feelings about Cardigan are mixed, aren't they?"

Kacey stopped pacing. "I suppose so," she answered after a few seconds. "He and I disagree on just about everything—but I don't know. Right now, yes, I'm really looking forward to seeing him again."

"That's how I feel about most of the men I get seriously mixed up with."

"Oh, I'm not really involved with Jake. It's more—"

"Kacey!" Rebecca was staring out into the darkening night.

"What is it?" She hurried over to the window.

"One of the guards isn't there anymore." Rebecca pointed.

Down below, the trees and the brush were swaying with increasing intensity and the sound of the wind was growing.

"You mean the guy who was stationed in that stand of palm trees?" asked Kacey.

"There's no sign of him. I just noticed."

"Could be he's taking a break." Kacey started to reach her stungun out of its holster.

A shattergun roared outside. The next viewindow over from them exploded, and thousands of glittering fragments of plasti-glass came cascading and spinning into the room.

Harsh wind came rushing in, too.

Next, two men leaped in through the fresh-made opening.

"What a happy occasion, Sis," said one of them. "I imagine you thought, you conniving bitch, that I'd gone on to my reward after you destroyed the goddamn Tek laboratory. You figured we'd never meet again in this world."

Taking a step back from her brother, Rebecca said, "I was sure as hell hoping you were dead, Rollo."

"Let go the gun." The bald man with the piping voice was prodding Kacey with the barrel of his lazrifle.

She complied, glaring at the man.

Burdon bowed in her direction. "What a pleasant surprise to

find you at our party, Miss Bascom," he said. "My fondness for any member of the Bascom family is almost as strong as my feelings for my dear sister." He walked closer to Rebecca and, with the hand that wasn't holding the lazgun, slapped her across the face. Hard, three times.

"Your pop hired lousy help to guard you," Summerson told Kacey. "Really easy to take out. A snap, actually, too easy to be much fun."

Burdon hit his sister twice more. As she fell back onto a low white sofa, he told her, "I never have much liked you, Becky. But, Jesus, now that you've developed this rudimentary moral sense, you're impossible."

"Rollo, you're not going to be able to salvage a damned thing," Rebecca said, rubbing at her bleeding cheek. "The Tek plant is done for. Out in NorCal they're probably already closing in on Zack Excoffon—and your name is starting to show up on a lot of police shit lists, dear."

"Plus which," added Kacey, "the SoCal cops are just about convinced you, and not my father, are responsible for the death of Dwight Grossman."

Rowland laughed. "You ladies don't understand the nature of revenge—the pure unadulterated kind," he said. "I didn't track you down and drop in tonight because I want to revive my fortunes."

The wind was even stronger now. It was invading the room, rattling everything, howling.

Burdon laughed again. "No, I'm here simply to kill you both."

THE WIND CAUGHT Gomez and gave him an immense shove.

He went sprawling and rolling down the hillside and came to rest close to where Jake was crouching and waiting for him.

"*Chihuahua,*" he said as Jake helped him get to a kneeling position.

"Are we set?" asked Jake.

"*Sí.* I just stungunned the last of the opposition guards. This damned wind makes it easy to sneak up on lunkheads and louts."

"Then we can move on up to the villa."

"Might as well, now that we've played our little game. They stun our guards, we arrive and stun theirs." Gomez rose up. "Inefficient, if you think about it. If there was a moratorium on guards, then we'd both save a lot of—"

"Onward and upward," suggested Jake, starting to climb the windswept hillside toward the beleaguered Villa Sombra.

THE WIND RUSHED into the living room, slapping at a floor lamp and toppling it.

Kacey dodged to keep from being hit by it.

She tried, as she lunged, to chop the lazrifle out of Summerson's grip.

"No chance, honey." He laughed a fluty laugh and easily avoided her.

She fell, her knee slamming into the carpeted floor.

As she started to get up, Kacey caught a flash of movement just outside the high, wide broken window.

Instead of continuing her rise, she dropped to the floor again and cried out in pain.

"What the hell's bothering you?" Summerson wanted to know.

"My ribs." She hugged herself, writhing on the floor and moaning. "I broke a couple of the damned things when I fell."

Bending, the bald man grabbed the back of her jacket and yanked. "Get your butt up off there."

At that same instant Gomez came diving into the room through the big opening where the window had been.

He landed on his side, went rolling across the floor, and came to his feet facing Burdon and with his stungun in his hand. He fired.

The first shot didn't connect.

Jake arrived then, tackling the distracted Summerson from behind.

Getting an armlock on the big bald man, Jake jerked him back and away from Kacey.

As Burdon swung his lazgun up to use on Gomez, Rebecca jumped from the sofa and threw herself into him. Her left shoulder hit him in the chest.

Burdon's lazgun went swinging way up in his hand, and the sizzling beam cut a sooty rut up the wall and partway across the ceiling.

Planting his legs wide, Gomez used his stungun again.

This time the beam took Burdon in the side. He gasped, staggered backwards. A strong blast of wind hit him in the back, shoving him forward again.

He seemed to freeze all at once, dropping his lazgun and falling over into a sparkling scatter of broken plastiglass.

Rebecca dived, grabbed up the lazgun, and aimed it at her brother.

"Don't," advised Gomez. "Not worth the trouble, *señorita.*"

She looked over at him, her mouth a thin angry line. Sighing, she said, "No, it isn't." She dropped the gun into her pocket.

Jake and Summerson meantime had ended up outside the living room. They were wrestling out in the brush on the hillside.

Summerson brought up his knee but failed to connect with Jake's chin.

Jake spun clear, stood, grabbed up the bald man, and hit him in the face. He did that three more times.

"This is for hurting my son," he said, hitting him yet again, hard, square in the face.

Summerson groaned, went slack.

Jake hit him twice more.

He let go and the big bald man dropped down into the high grass and the wind came roaring at him.

"You about finished up out there, *amigo?*" called Gomez from inside.

"Yeah. You?"

"Burdon's down and out."

Jake, none too carefully, dragged Summerson back into the living room and dropped him on the floor. "We can get out of here as soon as we dispose of these fellows."

Kacey, smiling, came over to him. "You were very impressive, Jake," she said, putting her arms around him and kissing him on the cheek. "Despite your narrow-minded views on politics, you're not a bad guy."

"Ah, then this was all worth it," he said, grinning.

"What say," put in Gomez, "we pack up and get off this island before the hurricane gets any worse?"

45 • JAKE,

alone, set his skycar down in the landing area of the Nutmeg Nature Preserve as twilight was beginning to fill the twenty-acre spread. It was an hour beyond closing time and there were no other vehicles on the lot.

He eased out of the car and went hurrying up a twisting gravel path that wound through a forest that was a blend of real and holographic trees, brush, and plants. Upon the branch of a real tree, a robot bird was singing.

"Welcome back to Connecticut, Mr. Cardigan," said a long, lean man in a plaid jacket and gray trousers who was standing at the side of the path with a double-barreled lazrifle cradled in his arms.

"Evening, Jason."

The caretaker nodded up the path. "Miss Pennoyer's been expecting you."

Nodding, Jake continued on his way.

There was a rural cabin at the path's end, and sitting on the porch was a woman. She was a shade over four feet tall and when she, smiling, left the low rocker, you saw that on her left foot she wore a built-up shoe. "Jake, it's been a while since you've dropped in on your lopsided friend."

"Three years, Maggie." He came up the real wood steps, took hold of both her hands, and bent to kiss her on the cheek. "You're looking fine."

"Fine as I'll ever look." Maggie Pennoyer led him into the front room of the cabin, where a real fire burned in a real fireplace. "Let me get rid of the basic stuff first off. My business is still thriving and the government doinks I used to work for still don't know where I'm based. Right at the moment I've got four other customers in residence in my rural sanitarium here. And I'm still dedicated to renovating people who've been mindwiped, brainwashed, and otherwise neurologically diddled with." She got herself seated on a plaid sofa. "Now you can ask me your questions."

He grinned. "How's my son?"

"That ham-handed Dr. Stolzer, you know, is a long way from being at the top of his class." Maggie rested her hands on her knees. "I've worked on a few of his victims over the years. He's a second-rate mindwiper, if that."

"Meaning?"

"Suppose you give your son a call," she suggested. "He's a lot cuter than you, by the way. Of course, if he lives a few more decades of the life you lead, he may turn out as weather-beaten and woebegone as you."

Jake crossed to the open doorway she was pointing at across

the room. Stopping on the threshold, he called out, "Dan? It's me."

Dan appeared in the doorway. He hesitated, then came into the warm room. "It's okay," he said, smiling. "I know who I am, I know who you are. Maggie got me back."

Jake put his arms around his son and hugged him. "Welcome back."

"Thanks, Dad."

Over his shoulder, Jake said, "Thanks, Maggie."